*EVEN A DOCTOR
BURIES HIS
MISTAKES...*

DOCTOR'S ORDERS

BY ALBERT KOVETZ, M.D.

M. L. "The point is," the reporter said with deliberate hesitation, "someone at your hospital is deliberately killing patients to cover up serious malpractice."

Burt had been a doctor for too long to accept the reporter's allegation, and he decided to challenge him: "Have you told anyone else about this, like the police, for instance?"

The reporter looked surprised. "Quite simply, I don't know which deaths are deliberate. How would it sound if I called the cops to tell them people are dying in the hospital? You see, that's where you come in," the reporter said, pounding the table with his fist.

The reporter was becoming too sure of himself, too sure that Burt would be willing to help. And they both knew that if Burt offered his assistance, there would be no turning back.

"Well," the reporter said impatiently, "will you help?"

Burt took a deep breath before answering.

FIRST-RATE ADVENTURES FOR MEN

DOCTOR'S ORDERS

BY ALBERT KOVETZ, M.D.

ZEBRA BOOKS
KENSINGTON PUBLISHING CORP.

ZEBRA BOOKS

are published by

KENSINGTON PUBLISHING CORP.
475 Park Avenue South
New York, N.Y. 10016

Printed in the United States of America

ONE

"I'll keep my gallbladder just where it is," Dr. Burt Josephson said as he unbuckled his belt to tuck his shirttails into his pants. The size forty-six tag on the inside flashed for a moment as he sucked in his ample belly.

"I didn't say you shouldn't," Dr. Nathan Simon corrected him, "I said that if you don't change your diet, you won't have any choice. Besides, we're not even sure the problem is your gallbladder."

"Of course it is. The symptoms are perfect. Right upper-quadrant pain brought on by a fatty meal. What kind of a doctor are you, anyway?" Josephson sneered.

He sat down on a round upholstered stool and leaned against the wall of the examining room, and crossed one leg over the other to tie his shoelace. As he bent forward, his white shirt bulged at the sides in smooth waves of flowing fat. He sat up, leaving his legs crossed.

"Did you ever go to medical school?" Josephson, slightly short of breath, needled tall, gangly Dr. Simon.

Before Simon could answer, Josephson's roly-poly leg slipped off his thigh. He lost his balance and the wheeled stool moved out from under him. He grabbed at the utility cabinet, but too late. His head bumped lightly against the plaster wall and he was unceremoniously dumped on his ass.

"Son of a bitch! I'm gonna sue you!" Josephson shook his head, slightly stunned and embarrassed.

"How can you sue me? This is your office, schmuck!" Simon chuckled as he helped Josephson back on his feet.

Nathan Simon extended his lean hand to Josephson. With remarkable ease, he pulled the two-hundred-and-fifty-pound Josephson to his feet. Dr. Simon had always been thin but athletically built with a wiry strength that surprised many people. At fifty, he weighed the same as he had in college.

He knew Dr. Burt Josephson before that. In fact, he couldn't remember a time when he hadn't known him. Sometime back in the thirties when kids still wore knickers with knee socks, a short cherubic Burt Josephson waddled alongside an intense bone-thin boy named Nathan Simon. Simon's socks looked as if they were starched around his legs and neatly tucked under the elastic of brown plaid knickers. Josephson never seemed to get the knack. His elastic was usually around the ankle, more often only one, as if he reveled in asymmetry. His shirttail was also a wandering wonder, perennially rejected from the inside of his pants.

Without conscious effort, they continued to walk in the same direction for nearly half a century. Josephson had managed to keep his shirttails in place, and a fifty-to-seventy-five-pound weight difference between him and Simon as well.

Simon's neat reserve had always made him look older. He would say "more mature" when it was desirable to look older. Now his hair was all white. Josephson had only a column of white along his sideburns, in contrast to his thick mound of curly black hair.

"It doesn't matter whose office it is," Josephson said as he placed the sliding stool out of harm's way. "you're still responsible for your patient."

"Oh, God!" Simon sighed. "If I had any patients like you my hair would be all white."

"You're just lucky we're friends. Otherwise you'd be in a lot of trouble," Josephson joked as he led Simon from the examining room to his consultation room. "What are you doing here, anyway?" he asked as he stretched back in his high-backed chair. Simon leaned against the front of the desk.

"I was going to ask you to play tennis with me tomorrow afternoon but now I'm not sure. How sick are you?" Simon questioned with cynical concern.

"That's what you're supposed to tell me, Doctor. You *are* a doctor?" Josephson sneered.

"I'm a doctor. Why can't you be like a patient? Call my office for an appointment and I'll take care of you properly. I really think you need a gallbladder series," Simon said sincerely.

"I need a gallbladder x-ray like a hole in the head," Josephson brushed away the suggestion with a wave of his hand. "Surgery is out of the question," he paused and then stared for a moment with a hang-dog look at his oldest friend. "Unless my eyes turn yellow. Then I'll consider it."

"Whatever you say. But do me a favor. Don't tell anyone you're my patient unless you show up at my office and behave like a patient. What about tennis tomorrow?"

"Oh, you'll never guess who called me," Josephson said exuberantly. Simon didn't even try to guess. It was obvious that Josephson was bursting with the news.

"Charlie Dresden," Josephson said, obviously expecting Simon to be impressed. He waited, but the desired reaction failed to come.

"Charlie Dresden, the newspaper reporter!" Josephson repeated, to strike a reponsive chord in Simon, who just stood there trying to figure out Josephson's excitement. "Don't you remember him? He went to school with us. In junior high, he was that weird-looking kid who grew a moustache in the eighth grade and got suspended because he refused to shave it off."

The association drew no blood from Simon who shifted his weight and narrowed his eyes trying to think of a twelve-year-old kid with a moustache.

"You remember him," Josephson was eager to jolt Simon's memory. "He sat in front of the third row right in front of Mrs. Latour with the big tits. He was very quiet."

"How the fuck do you remember who sat where almost forty years ago?" Simon asked with astonishment and chagrin. His own memory of that time was a blank compared to Burt Josephson's.

The name Charlie Dresden started to come back to him. He could picture the classroom. A cardboard alphabet lined the tops of blackboards in wooden frames; every classroom was so adorned in the days when penmanship was still drilled. The was also a flag sticking out from the wall.

He could picture the robust twelve-year-old Josephson squeezing his stomach between the seat and desk in a row of desk-seat combinations. They were oak seats and desk tops held by curved wrought iron legs bolted to the floor. He pictured Josephson struggling to turn back in his seat to signal to him when the teacher wasn't looking. A few other faces and names flooded his memory but Charlie Dresden remained a moustache without any other features.

"I remember where he sat," Burt Josephson explained, "because his head was always blocking Mrs. Latour's tits. She used to wear those low-cut dresses and when she leaned forward I thought I could look into heaven."

"Is he in the high-school yearbook? I'd remember him if I saw his picture," Simon said.

"No, he quit high school or was kicked

out. He joined the Marines. After that he went to college. I told you about him once before. He's a pretty famous reporter, sort of a war correspondent or something. His byline was in The New York Times. I showed it to you."

"Oh, yeah, you did," Simon suddenly remembered, "but it didn't mean anything then and I still can't put a face to that name. Listen, I've got to go. Can you play tennis tomorrow?"

"No, that's what I've been trying to tell you," Josephson said with a quiet smile. "Charlie wants me to meet him for lunch tomorrow in New York."

Besides being warm and genuinely interested in his fellow human beings, Burt Josephson harbored a fantasy in which he was a confidante to the famous people of the world. He did not imagine an acquired intimacy based on some mutual exchange in business. He felt there was no way for him to enter the inner circles of strangers who had acquired fame. Except for his obscurity, which he always expected and accepted with equanimity, his life was full, rich and satisfying.

Burt never told Nathan Simon the real reason he remembered Charlie. Around 1960, Charlie called Burt's office. At first, the name meant nothing to Burt until

11

Charlie mentioned Mrs. Latour's tits. Of course, that jogged Burt's memory and they reminisced about those two globes for a while.

Charlie wanted to see Burt about a medical problem which turned out to be a case of the clap. Burt fixed him up while they waxed nostalgic and eventually got around to discussing Charlie's career. Burt was impressed because Charlie had just finished a series of articles on Indochina. Burt had read the articles without knowing the author. But there it was in black and white. Charles Dresden, the twelve-year-old kid with the moustache, had broken into print.

It was nearly another twenty years before he heard from Charlie Dresden again but in the interim he had looked carefully for his byline. During the Viet-Nam War, he had seen it often but more recently it had become rare.

When Charlie called to ask Burt to lunch, Burt had no trouble remembering who he was. He had said to keep in touch and time plays tricks on the mind. It seemed like he had seen him yesterday.

"Burt," Charlie said with charming enthusiasm, "I'll be in New York for a few weeks."

"Well, come out to Jersey for the weekend. You know, Nathan Simon is out here, too," Burt interrupted. "A lot of people you knew are here. We could have a high-school reunion.''

"That sounds great and I'd really love to," Charlie said, "but I just don't have the time. I'm here on special assignment. It has a medical angle and I'd like to get your views on it. Could you meet me for lunch? Noon at the Perigord.''

"In New York?" Burt hesitated for a moment. "That'll be great. Where is it?''

"New York? Where it's always been," Charlie laughed.

"I mean the restaurant," Burt explained.

"Fifty-third or fifty-fourth. I'll see you there Thursday and give my best to Sy.''

"Sy? Who's Sy?" Burt asked. There was a moment of embarrassing silence. "You mean Nate Simon! Nate Simon.''

"Right! I'll see you Thursday." Charlie hung up.

Burt was married to Loretta, a woman whose charm and beauty had matured elegantly since they first met in high school thirty years earlier. Like Nathan Simon, she was, in physical appearance, the antithesis of Burt Josephson. About five feet six inches tall, she never weighed more than one hundred fifteen pounds except when she was pregnant. Out of that came two grown sons whom Burt loved dearly.

He had forgotten to tell Loretta about the lunch date. On Thursday morning, he felt it would be a mistake to go off to New

York without telling her even though it was only an hour away.

"I'm going to New York to have lunch today," he said as he sipped his morning orange juice while Loretta prepared his usual breakfast of scrambled eggs, bacon and toast.

"I thought something was different. That explains your new suit." Loretta observed.

Burt had turned out in a three-piece suit of light tan gabardine. It was quite different from the casual sport coat and often crumpled pants that Loretta had to sneak away to send to the cleaner. Today he looked more like a banker than a doctor—and a very prosperous one if girth were a measure of wealth. The vest made him hold in his stomach, contributing to his imposing appearance.

"Don't you want to know why I'm going?" he demanded when it appeared Loretta would not ask. She sat down to sip her coffee indifferently.

"Sure, but first I want to know if I can go with you. I've begged you a million times to take an afternoon off for a matinee or something. What magnet is pulling you there today?"

Burt had to admit to himself that she had a point. It would kill two birds with one stone. He felt guilty about why he had forgotten to tell her before this: he didn't want to share Charlie with her.

"I'm being interviewed by a reporter," Burt said modestly.

"That's marvelous!" Loretta said. Whenever she was moved her pale blue eyes seemed to get darker. "About what? For what?" she started excitedly. "Will it be on television?"

"No, it's a newspaper reporter. Charlie Dresden. I told you about him, it was—my gosh, it was some time ago," Burt said.

Loretta picked up the plates from the table in the dining area of the kitchen. It was a comfortable house that they had bought fifteen years before. It was much too large for only the two of them. Both their sons were grown. One was a lawyer and the other was in medical school.

"I can meet you there if you'll be too tied up to pick me up or I can meet you at your office." Loretta said eagerly.

"I'll pick you up at ten-thirty, right here," Burt conceded. As he pushed himself away from the table, his abdomen bumped against the table's edge. The buttons on his vest were severely strained.

"First tell me what it's all about," Loretta smiled. "Why are you being interviewed, and what? Come on! Don't make me drag every bit out of you."

"I don't know what it's about," Burt sighed, knowing he had emphasized the interview aspect too much. "Charlie Dresden called me a few days ago and simply asked me to meet him for lunch."

"Who's Charlie Dresden?" Loretta asked.

Burt shifted his feet and leaned against the back of the chair. His cheeks puffed out and then he let the air out silently through pursed lips.

"If I didn't love you so much, I could get angry with you very easily," he sighed. "How many times have I told you about Charlie? I know you read the newspapers. You must have seen his name."

While Burt simmered his slow burn, Loretta ran over to him. In her bare feet, she had to stand on tip-toes to kiss his ear. She did it sensuously, knowing how much he would like it. It always turned his mood. Her arms extended around his girth but couldn't meet by a foot or more. He squirmed without pulling away.

"Tell me again about Charlie Dresden," she said happily, as happy to be loving him as he was for her to continue.

"Okay, if you'll stop doing that for a second, I'll tell you."

She stopped but still held on to him.

"Maybe I'll just stay home until ten-thirty," He put his around her; it seemed they could go around twice.

"No, sir!" she said, feeling she was in control. "Tell me about Charlie Dresden."

"He went to Sixty-Six, to school with me and Nate. Now he's a reporter with The

New York Times. I showed you his bylines years ago when he was with the A.P. or some other news service."

"But that was years ago. How could you expect me to remember?"

"It wasn't so long ago," Burt insisted.

"Wait a minute," Loretta said squirming out of his grip. She walked around the table. "I don't think I'll go after all."

"Why?"

"Why? Because it's going to deteriorate into a story-telling contest about Sixty-Six. Whenever you and Nate meet someone from that school, I hear the same old stories and they get worse and worse. I can tell them as well as you can by now. And I'm getting tired of them!"

"It's not that bad," Burt said defensively. "Besides, Nate won't be there, so why don't you come? Really. I really want you to meet Charlie."

"No, you go ahead. In this case, I'm sure you'll have a much better time without me," Loretta said honestly.

"If you're sure," Burt said, still feeling guilty.

TWO

Dr. Josephson had carefully arranged his day. The office was closed. Nathan Simon would take any urgent calls but Burt had ample time to make rounds and see his patients in the hospital. Those patients wouldn't even know he was gone unless there was some unexpected crisis in their illness, but he had to let them know Simon was covering, just in case.

Brady Memorial Hospital, where Josephson admitted his patients, was named after Henry Justin Brady. The original hospital was paid for by the Brady family in honor of their son, who crashed his biplane during pilot training in 1917.

The hospital, a square, three-story building of tan brick with forty beds was opened in 1922. It was an ostentatious monument and too large for the rural community at the time. For thirty years, it remained unchanged and under-utilized.

Then the rush to suburbia began and the Brady Memorial Hospital grew, sporadically at first, with a small wing here and a new room there. In 1960, a completely new three-hundred-bed hospital was built, dwarfing the old structure. The community was proud of its efforts. The Brady name stuck even though the original family had disappeared from the area in the thirties. It was rumored that their wealth was dissipated in the crash of '29.

Dr. Josephson began his rounds with two patients in the Intensive Care Unit. In the first cubicle he entered, accompanied by nurse Joan Chimento, 94-year-old Elizabeth Bentley was sitting propped up with two pillows against the raised head of the hospital bed. She was alert, thin, and the rimless glasses pressed against her pinched nose seemed like fine crystal glass.

A green oxygen hose was suspended inside her nose by two prongs.

She looked up at Josephson as if she would like to give him a tongue-lashing. When she was able to speak, she was interrupted by gasps and difficult breathing. It markedly reduced the impact of her words.

"Have you—any more—damned tubes to stick—in me?" she demanded.

"Talk a little more slowly," the nurse advised her as she rearranged the pillows which had fallen low on the bed.

Joan Chimento was a tall thin woman with high sharp cheekbones that accentuated her almond-shaped eyes. She looked like a young girl but was actually thirty-eight and had two grown children. As she plumped the pillows and lifted Mrs. Bentley to a more comfortable position, she gave the old woman a hug.

Mrs. Bentley said, "Stop fussin' with me, girlie," but she was now obviously more comfortable and could speak more easily. "I'm sorry, love," she reconsidered and pursed her lips in regret, "I'm just not used to bein' fussed over so much. I though I'd rather die than face the day when I couldn't make my own bed."

"You're doing much better than when you were brought in twelve hours ago," Josephson said looking at her chart. He placed a stethoscope on her back and asked her to breathe in and out several times. She was calmer and breathed more easily.

"Still a way to go," the doctor said, "but not bad for an old lady who didn't need digitalis until your age."

"Never mind my age," she said slowly but still managing to demonstrate a little vanity. "What are you all dressed up for? Takin' Miss Joanie out for lunch?" she grinned devilishly, exposing a perfect row of false teeth.

Josephson couldn't help blushing. Joan Chimento was very beautiful and he had "lusted in his heart" as did practically every doctor on the staff when it came to Joan. More than a few had lusted beyond the heart but, as far as Burt knew, no one had gotten very far with her.

Joan Chimento was the nurse in charge of the Intensive Care Unit. She knew all the patients admitted there. She was also the buffer between her staff of nurses, who manned the Unit around the clock every day of the year, and the individual physicians and surgeons who admitted patients there.

It was her personality which calmed the flames of indignation when things didn't go quite as the doctor expected. More often than not, a problem was due to a lack of communication between doctor and nurse, sometimes between doctor and doctor. When the patient had more than one doctor, Joan would smooth the ruffled feathers and soothe hurt egos. An old saying goes: If a patient has one doctor, there is a chance of recovery. If there are two doctors, the outcome is in doubt. When three doctors are involved, there is no hope at all. The Intensive Care Unit was more efficient because of Joan's intervention.

Joan attached herself to Burt Josephson's elbow in response to Mrs. Bentley's teasing; it was as if a white pencil had been attached to the side of a tan clipboard. She was tall and thin. Her white blouse hung loosely over her white pants and hid the curves of her soft round hips. She pressed against the side of the taller, broader Josephson, who blushed even further.

"Well, what do you think, Elizabeth?" Joan said with a cheerful smile that brought a starburst around her eyes. "How do we go together?"

Elizabeth Bentley threw back her head and laughed silently. Burt looked down at Joan Chimento with a frown brought out by embarrassment rather than reproof.

"Where are you going?" Joan said standing away from him, looking up and down, sizing up the cut of his coat. She nodded approvingly.

"Why must I be going any place just because I wear a suit for a change?" Josephson asked.

"With a suit like that, you're going either to a Bar Mitzvah or a funeral. And since it's Thursday, it can't be a Bar Mitzvah and I don't know anyone you know who died," Joan said.

"You'd feel rotten if I told you someone died," Burt said. Immediately, he saw the remorse creep into Joan's face. Perhaps she had overstepped her intimacy.

"Well, relax. I'm having lunch with a very famous person in New York," Burt assured her. "You can't come," he said stabbing her for her presumptions. "Mrs. Bentley, everything is fine. A day or two more in this unit and I think you can be moved to a regular room. It wasn't too serious. Too much salt and too much fluid in your lungs. The medication will make you as good as you were before you got sick. I'll see you tomorrow."

"Doctor, could we get rid of this thing in my arm?" Mrs. Bentley pleaded as she pointed to the intravenous line running into her left forearm.

"In a couple of days," Josephson said. He walked out of the cubicle, followed by nurse Chimento.

The Intensive Care Unit had ten cubicles arranged around the periphery of a square room with the nurses' station at the center. There was a bank of oscilloscopes at the station fed by satellite scopes at the head of each bed. The patients' privacy was penetrated by electronic gadgetry and glass doors. That was the function of intensive care.

The room reminded Josephson of another hospital room that was perhaps the same size as this one. The bed arrangement was the same but there were thirty beds lined against the walls of an open ward at Kings County Hospital.

That was twenty-five years earlier and the open ward permitted a few nurses to observe a lot a patients without electronic devices. As an intern, he always found the yellow-white room with its peeling paint depressing. The shiny electronic Intensive Care Unit made him recognize the utilitarian value of the old hospital's design.

Sad as those figures of human suffering might have appeared, sitting or lying in open beds and seen by whoever walked by, they were never lonely. Even without electronics, they could get help immediately when they needed it.

In so many ways, electronics has isolated one human being from another, he reflected. It has created a two-dimensional world without sweat or smells, a world without substance. The same kinds of probes that have endangered the world's privacy are used to give the appearance of privacy in the hospital. It affords privacy and the price is loneliness.

"Has Klein seen her yet?" Josephson stopped short. Dr. Klein was a cardiologist and Dr. Josephson had asked for a consultation when it looked like Mrs. Bentley had a serious problem. Chimento, close behind Dr. Josephson, stumbled over his heels.

"Most Mack trucks have tail lights for sudden stops," she quipped. Josephson ignored her remark.

"Has he been in yet?" he asked again.

"He saw her quickly," Chimento said. "She seemed to be doing well but he said he'd be back this afternoon and might put in a Schwan-Ganz," she said flatly.

Josephson twisted his chubby face, leaving no doubt that he didn't like the idea at all. It was just the thing Mrs. Bentley complained about: another tube. This one would go in her arm, through the veins, pass through two chambers of her heart and out to the arteries going to the lungs.

Sometimes it was valuable if it wasn't possible to tell the difference between heart failure and shock, or if a patient with severe heart disease needed lots of fluids. The tube was one thing Mrs. Bentley didn't need. There was no doubt about her diagnosis and she was responding very well to Josephson's therapy.

"Can I cancel the consultation?" Josephson asked sheepishly.

"Too late for that," she said, knowing he wouldn't anyway. "He's already written a note on the chart."

"Well, don't let him do it," he said.

"You want me to tell Dr. Klein what he

25

can or cannot do?'' Nurse Chimento asked, eyes wide in disbelief at his request.

"You can do it. Flutter those blue eyes at him and he'll do anything you say.'' Josephson was hopeful, but Chimento was not about to accept such a verbal order.

"I'll write it on the chart,'' Burt said. "I don't want her Schwaned!''

He took a deep breath so his pants slipped a little. He pulled them back over his hips.

"Maybe I don't want to put that on the chart,'' he said reconsidering. "He'll think I'm telling him what to do, which he'll take much worse from me than if you tell him. Damn! I wish I could be here. Listen, if he wants to Schwan her, call Dr. Simon. He'll be covering for me this afternoon.''

"Don't worry,'' she assured him. "He won't do it. I can't spare anyone to help him set up and he won't do it with the three-to-eleven shift unless it's an emergency.

"So, what's with this big date you have in New York? Anybody I know?'' she smiled and raised her eyebrows.

"If you read the New York Times regularly, you would know him. At least recognize the name,'' he said.

"Well, pardon me?'' she said sarcastically.

"I'll see you in the funny papers, kiddo,'' he said with a jolly wink.

26

THREE

Burt Josephson pulled his big, five-year-old blue Buick Electra out of the toll gate of the George Washington Bridge. Lately, he felt the stigma of driving the big gas guzzler but it ran well and the extra five miles per gallon he might get from a newer, smaller car didn't seem worth it. Someone had called it The Blue Max, which didn't make much sense except that it was blue. Still, the name stuck in his mind and he liked it. It had an aura of nostalgia. Keep it, he was told. Someday it will be a classic. Bullshit! He'd run it into the ground and then junk it.

He crossed the bridge on the upper roadway so he could see the towering lattice of symmetrical steel towers, the river below and the city beyond.

Josephson tried to be both physician and friend to his patients. He liked Mrs. Bentley, with her fragile independence. At her best, she could make the world stand on its head, but it took so little to knock her off balance.

He liked Mrs. Bentley because she trusted his judgment and his physical findings more than the results of any laboratory test or electronic device. In the twenty-five years since he had graduated from medical school, Burt Josephson had seen dramatic changes in the way medicine was practiced. Unfortunately, he felt the cutting edge of that progress was the transistor and fiberoptics.

He liked gadgets just as much as the next man. An electronic thermometer that gave a digital readout of 98.5 was more precise but only a mock progression from a glass mercury thermometer that could only be read to the closest two tenths of a degree. What difference did it make if the patient's temperature was 98.5 or 98.6?

He stayed on the expressway across the upper neck of Manhattan to the F.D.R. Drive, then headed downtown. He watched the East River as much as he did the roadway. Traffic was light. He recited from memory the sequence of bridges over the East River to Long Island: Throg's Neck, Whitestone, Triborough, Queensborough, Williamsburg, Manhattan, Brooklyn.

In absent thought and stream of consciousness as he drove, the names mixed rhythmically and blasphemously with an ancient Hebraic prayer: . . . *and thou shalt teach them diligently unto thy children, and shalt speak of them when thou sittest in thine house, and when thou walkest by the way and when thou liest down and when thou risest up.*

It was a case of time playing tricks, time mixing things learned long ago. Contemporary synapses activated deep in the cortex wrapped in the same time-frame.

Otherwise why should he teach anyone the sequences of bridges? To prove he was a native New Yorker? Remember the movie where they asked the German spy suspect, "Who played third base for the Yankees in 1939?"

"I don't know. Please give me a break. I was a Dodger fan, ya gotta believe me!"

"No dice! It's the Yankees or nothin. Plug him."

"No! Please give me a break. I don't like baseball but I'm still an American. Ask me anything else!"

"Okay, this is your last chance. Name the bridges over the East River, from south to north in sequence. One mistake and we plug you."

"Okay. Brooklyn, Manhattan, Williamsburg, Queensborough, Triborough, Whitestone and Throgs Neck."

"What was that last one?"

"Throgs Neck."

"Plug the Kraut. I never hoid of it."

"No! Wait! They're going to build it after the war. Honest!"

He drove past the exit he wanted. The next one was close by and he got to the restaurant, even with the difficulty of finding a place to park, a little before noon. Loretta was right. They should come to the city more often. It took less than an hour when traffic was light.

Josephson's apprehension dissipated momentarily when he stepped into the restaurant. Somehow he expected something more extravagant, perhaps waterfalls and torches or mirrors that challenged the grandeur of Versailles. Instead he found a tastefully reserved decor, simple white tablecloths against a blue background and blue linen.

The room was almost empty except for two occupied tables in the rear of the room. It was five minutes to noon. A tall, sharp-nosed man came up to him quickly. Burt was impressed that he wore a tuxedo at noon.

"May I help you, monsieur?" he queried in a version of a French accent which Burt failed to detect was false. It just made him nervous.

"Er—I'm here to meet Charlie Dresden," Burt stammered scanning the near-empty room.

"Pardon, monsieur?" the maitre d' looked haughtily straight into Burt's face. Burt turned to meet the impertinent gaze.

"I'm Dr. Josephson," Burt stared back. "I have a lunch date here with Mr. Dresden. Charles Dresden of The Times."

"Ah, Dr. Josephson, your table is ready. Right this way."

He led Burt to a table just beyond the velvet rope and held a chair for him. He held the chair, but not quite far enough away from the table. As Burt sat down, he bumped the table hard with his belly and knocked over the vase holding a single rose. An attentive waiter immediately restored the vase and straightened the silverware before it was barely noticed.

He sat facing the entrance. He wished Charlie were there so he wouldn't have to deal with the maitre d'.

"May I get you a drink? Perhaps some white wine?" the maitre d' hovered about the table, accompanied by two other men in short blue waistcoats. Everything that was furniture or background was either blue or white.

To drink before noon would never have occurred to Burt. He rarely drank except at parties and special occasions. He certainly didn't want to before his meeting with Charlie since he wasn't used to it. Burt declined, but the maitre d' insisted in the way one does at home when a dear and valued friend drops in.

"We have an exquisite dry chablis, monsieur. I picked it out myself. You will love it. It will tingle on your tastebuds."

Burt shook his head but the maitre d' held his hurt feelings on his sleeve. Burt felt he was insulting the man's hospitality. He relented and ordered a scotch sour he really didn't want. One of the blue coated men instantly disappeared to fetch it. The cloud lifted from the maitre d's face.

Resolution of this stalemate relieved the siege at the table. Burt relaxed a bit as he drummed his fingers on the table. It was uncomfortable to turn around to look at the people dining at the far corner of the room.

Charlie Dresden appeared at the velvet rope where he was greeted by the maitre d'. Charlie pointed the way to Burt and was escorted to the table. Burt would never have recognized him. It had been twenty years since he saw him and then it had been but twenty minutes. The face he remembered and associated with Charlie Dresden was that of a twelve-year-old kid with a moustache.

The face Burt saw was narrow with the skin drawn tightly around thin lips. It was mature but still unwrinkled. Charlie had the strange combination of a pale but ruddy complexion, perhaps due to the redness filtering through his hair. And he had no moustache.

Twenty years ago, Burt recalled quite distinctly, Charlie had worn a bushy, dark moustache. He didn't remember the redness in the hair. It was a dark red, almost brown, but now what struck him was the thinness of his upper lip without the moustache.

Burt recognized Charlie's walk. It hadn't changed in forty years. He ambled on his heels, letting his toes point outward with each step. It was an open gait in which he bounced with each footfall. When he reached the table, Burt recognized the way his hair at the neck curled toward the ear. That, too, had remained the same.

Charlie was a head shorter than either Burt or the maitre d'. He was thin from front to back but broad-shouldered and straight. His suit was a dark gray check, well-tailored and tapered to his thin waist. His bulging pockets were stuffed with papers and notes.

"Dr. Josephson," Charlie nodded with an outstretched hand and a tight-lipped smile, his thin upper lip pressed against his teeth. His grip was hard and powerful even over Burt's large meaty hands.

"Charlie. It's good to see you again," Burt said, half rising as Charlie sat down.

"Good to see you, Burt," Charlie replied, spreading a napkin over his lap.

When the maitre d' asked Charlie if he wanted a drink in the same way he had asked Burt, Charlie said no and moved his left arm across the table with an open palm, like a horizontal karate chop. The maitre d' disappeared without another word. Burt took note of the maneuver.

"How is Loretta?" Charlie asked as he reached into his shirt pocket to pull out a cigarette.

"Fine. She almost came with me today," Burt said. He was pleased Charlie remembered her name even though he had never met Loretta. Burt was sorry she hadn't come along. He was very proud of her.

Burt remarked on how far Charlie literally had gone from Brooklyn as he ticked off datelines from around the world associated with Charlie's name over the years. Charlie shrugged modestly and was complimentary to Burt.

The maitre d' insisted that Burt have an appetizer after the first meek refusal. He strongly recommended the hot clams with butter and garlic sauce. Burt's mouth watered and he was sorely tempted. He was concerned about his possible gallbladder condition. Because Nathan Simon was tentative about the diagnosis, Burt hesitated. Maybe he could blame Nate.

He was about to say no in the way Charlie dismissed the pressure to order a drink when Charlie spoke up and sided with the management. He who hesitates is lost, Burt conceded. He also ordered broiled filet of sole with mustard sauce, to everyone's approval. Charlie had the sole but declined the clams. Their gastronomy secure, Charlie got right to the point of the meeting.

"Why do doctors commit malpractice?" Charlie asked cheerfully.

Burt was amused and looked as cheerful as Charlie did. It was a trick question, he thought, like why do you beat your wife? Burt chuckled softly while trying to think of alternative meanings. The way Charlie said it could also mean a premeditated felony.

"Doctors don't set out to commit malpractice," Burt said, patronizing Charlie more than he intended. Charlie wasn't offended, if he noticed at all. His face showed a mixture of surprise and curiosity that made Burt go on.

"There is no such thing as statutory malpractice," Burt said pedantically. "It doesn't exist until a jury decides in favor of the plaintiff. And a jury's idea of malpractice is often quite different from that of the medical profession."

"But there are bad results," Charlie reminded Burt, cocking his head to one side.

"Some are better, some are worse," Burt agreed, "but the results don't correlate with malpractice. A good result never comes to trial even if there was malpractice along the way. A bad result can be the best of a terrible situation."

"Forget the sophistry," Charlie waved a fork at him. "A murder is still a murder whether or not the killer is convicted."

"That's true," Burt started to say as the waiter brought the food. He waited until the plates were set. "A bad result is not proof of malpractice anymore than a dead body is proof of murder."

"It's a good place to start," Charlie readjusted the napkin on his lap with a snap. "Malpractice doesn't produce good results."

The garlic sauce and the clams were delicious but Burt felt a little twinge in his abdomen. He couldn't tell if it was Charlie's attitude or his gallbladder that distressed him. He wiped a bit of butter from his chin, sorely tempted to dip some bread in the sauce, but pushed his plate away instead. Charlie was challenging him for some reason. The reporter wasn't eating so Burt decided to concentrate, also. Besides, it was probably better for his stomach.

"If you want to stick to generalities, then I have to agree with you," Burt said. "But remember, there are many professions that grant the title 'Doctor' and they are each judged by different standards. Chiropractors have very limited liability for diagnosis, for instance. If you judge a chiropractor by the standards of the medical doctors, then they would all be guilty of malpractice."

"Keep to your own profession," Charlie stubbed out his cigarette. Burt noticed the tobacco stains on his fingertips but restrained the urge to tell him to quit. "Can you think of an example where a deliberate act of malpractice leads to a good result?"

"First, a short lesson in anatomy so we can speak the same language," Burt said leaning forward on the table. "Do you know what a femur is?"

"Sure. That's the thigh bone. And the thigh bone's connected to the hip bone, now hear the word of the Lord! Go on."

"Very good. Now all the bones have bumps and grooves where the muscles attach. There are two called the trochanter on the femur, a lesser trochanter and a greater trochanter. That's not important.

37

Just keep the trochanter in mind.

"A healthy man consults physician after physician complaining of pain in his thigh. Examinations, laboratory tests, x-rays all fail to reveal any abnormality. There is actually nothing wrong with him. Some physicians reassure him, others prescribe drugs or physical therapy, but he is not satisfied with the diagnosis. Arthritis, myalgia, bursitis are all too commonplace for him to accept. They have no glamour and are hardly worth talking about.

"After a few years and many doctors, he finds a doctor who tells him there's a trochanter on his femur. He reacts with a mixture of relief and suspicion. A trochanter on a femur sounds exciting. It sounds rare, exotic, very dramatic. Best of all the doctor recommends surgery to cure it. It sounds good but he is not entirely convinced so he seeks one more opinion.

"Armed with the sublime knowledge about a trochanter on his femur, he lets the next doctor muddle about. When this doctor fails to even mention the trochanter, the patient prompts him.

"Do you think there might be a trochanter on my femur?" he proudly reveals this diagnostic gem to the befuddled practitioner.

"The doctor frowns momentarily as he considers this strange question. Remember the normal anatomy!

" 'Of course you have a trochanter on your femur,' the doctor says.

"The previous doctor is a genius in the eyes of his patient. He discovered a malady of which the patient can be proud. The patient returns to this genius and agrees to let him remove the troublesome trochanter. After surgery, the patient walks with a limp but no longer complains and no longer haunts doctors's offices.

"His body sways from side to side, up and down, as he proudly displays his disability while praising the doctor who discovered what had eluded half of medical science."

Burt finished his story and waited for a response from Charlie who was lighting up another cigarette.

"That's what I mean," Charlie said blowing smoke through his nose and pressing his upper lip against his teeth. "What makes doctors do things like that?"

"For God sakes, Charlie, that was a fable," Burt said showing great annoyance at Charlie's obtuseness. "I should have told you about Foxy-loxy so you'd get the point!"

"The point is," Charlie said with deliberate hesitation, "Someone at your hospital is deliberately killing the patients."

"That's not malpractice. That's murder!" Burt said as if it were an academic argument. He reacted as if he were making debate points. A moment later, he realized Charlie wasn't debating.

"Somebody is killing the patients?" Burt asked in disbelief.

"Somebody is deliberately killing to cover up serious malpractice," Charlie said stiffly as he pointed his cigarette at Burt, who could not accept the allegation.

"Have you told anyone else about this, like the police, for instance?" Burt challenged him.

"We're not ready for that yet," Charlie stated as the waiter placed the main course on the table. Burt waited anxiously for him to leave. He was afraid to let even a bit of this conversation go beyond them. In fact, he wished it had never started.

"Why not?" he questioned softly.

"Quite simply, I don't know which deaths in the hospital are deliberate. How would it sound if I called the cops to tell them there are people dying in the hospital?" Charlie complained as he relished his finely broiled sole.

"That's right!" Burt insisted, as if it settled the whole matter. He had lost his appetite.

"That's where you come in," Charlie said lightly pounding the table with the heel of his fist. Burt was startled.

"You've lost me, Charlie," Burt said shaking his head, "You're coming on very strong with something that makes no sense to me at all."

"I know, but there's a reason for it," Charlie said. He pushed his plate away after finishing the last morsel. Burt hadn't touched his fish at all.

"I had to have some idea where you stand, how you think. I didn't want to let this out if I couldn't trust you. I don't have anything solid to go on. Not yet. All I have is an anonymous tip. I recognized the name of your hospital. That's why I called you."

"It's ridiculous," Burt dismissed the notion. "Nothing like that could happen with all the committees and audits that go on in the hospital."

"You proved to me it's not impossible." Charlie said.

"That was just a bullshit story I made up," Burt was indignant. "You maneuvered me into it. That doesn't prove a thing."

"It proves you have an open and imaginative mind. That's all I ask, an open mind which realizes that we're only at the beginning of this thing. Just look at what goes on at the hospital with this possibility in mind. If you come up with anything, call me or leave a message for me at the paper. They'll know how to reach me. Okay? And when I get some facts, I'll let you know."

Burt didn't know what to say, and Charlie didn't give him a chance to sort out the situation. He stood up, said something about an urgent appointment and left Burt in a daze.

The maitre d' came over with the bill. Burt handed him his American Express card. He signed for the bill but was too preoccupied to be concerned with the three-figure total.

FOUR

Loretta came into the kitchen carrying two small bundles of groceries. She was wearing a white tennis dress with ruffles on the panties exposed behind. Her legs were slim, well-shaped and unmarked by age.

Burt was at the kitchen table, sitting over a large bowl heaped with cottage cheese, sour cream and a mixture of fresh fruits he had found in the refrigerator. He wore a checked shirt open at the collar, dungarees with a thick leather belt crowned with a large - buckle decorated with a Texas longhorn.

"What happened to your lunch date?" Loretta asked as she emptied the groceries from the bags to the shelves.

"Hmpf," Burt snorted with a mouth full of white mush. It was almost a snort, quite unpleasant, as it was meant to be.

"Stood up, huh?" she shrugged. "So were we. Marjorie Kaplan couldn't make it so we were left with a threesome for doubles."

Burt shoveled another spoonful into his mouth. He twisted his head from side to side in obvious agitation. Loretta ignored the disturbing sign in hope it would pass or he would tell her when he was ready.

"I didn't care. Tennis is getting to be so boring." she said. "Do you think I should go back to work?"

He swallowed and wiped his lips with a paper napkin. "I told you to last year," he sounded angry, but for an entirely different reason. "Why don't you come to work for me?"

"Being an office nurse is boring." she said. "Besides, you're too cheap."

"What difference does it make?" he demanded, letting his annoyance with Charlie Dresden take over. He gripped his spoon with a clenched fist. "It all goes into a joint account, anyway." He attacked the diminishing mound of cheese and fruit, stabbing hard with the spoon.

"That's another thing! I want my own money in my own account so I can be an individual, a person of my own," she said in a rising voice struggling for control.

"So what am I, chopped liver?" he said surprised at the intensity of the request. "Go ahead, put all the money in your name. I don't care. Just leave some for the office and the IRS. They're part of our joint account, too."

"It's not the money, Burt," she explained apologetically. "I have to have my own identity, independent of you. I had a career once. I was a pretty damned good nurse once upon a time."

"You were a beautiful nurse," Burt said lovingly. "You were gorgeous and you can still fit into your old uniforms."

"Ecch!" she said, making a sour face. "Those baggy dresses were like tents. I like those new styles. Nurses can wear whatever they like: tight, loose, slacks. The girls look terrific. Haven't you noticed?"

Burt ignored the cattiness of her last question. He was thinking about the problem Charlie had laid in his lap. He wanted to share it with Loretta so he could get her opinion, which he valued very much. First he had to get this bee out of her bonnet to get her attention.

"You could go back to the hospital but don't expect to start at the top." he said. "They need nurses but it's on shift and from eleven to seven."

"I know. What would you do without me at night?" she said sadly. "We'd never see each other," she said and went over to put her arms around his shoulders.

"Whatever you want," Burt said softly.

"It's not just that. I've been out of it so long. There are so many new methods, machines, different ways of doing things," she reflected, and walked off away from him dejectedly.

"Don't worry about that," Burt encouraged her. "People are still the same. You were a terrific nurse because you cared about people and you are very smart. You still have that. You can be taught about machines in a week. Remember the first television set your folks got in 1947? All those dials that only your father could touch. You were terrified to turn a knob so we sat there with the vertical going flip-flop for an hour until he got home."

Loretta smiled and blushed a bit even now as she recalled how she screamed at Burt as his hand went to the knob of her father's precious machine. Burt had stilled the picture with the "vertical" knob but she insisted he turn it back. It was if she believed her father had made a mark on the old TV set.

"You really think I can do it!" she exclaimed. "You don't think I'm too old to start learning again. Of course I'm not too old," she said indignantly. "You know what I mean, all those little girls just getting out of nurses' training."

"What are you talking about?" he said softening her ego. "Put your hair up in a pony tail and you can tell everyone you're my daughter. Just swish a little when you walk. You know Joan Chimento started the School of Nursing after she was thirty and now she's in charge of the ICU."

"Did she swish her way into that job?" Loretta was just a little bit angry in defense of the working woman and just a little bit jealous in defense of her perogatives.

"No, she's bright, sensible and beautiful, the way you are." Burt said proudly, "and if she could do it, so can you. You already have the skills and the degree."

"I really mean it and if you think I can, oh, Burt, it will feel so good," she smiled happily. He had accepted it so easily. "What about you? What happened today?"

She sat down at the table with Burt and listened quietly. He recounted his meeting with Charlie Dresden in every detail— except for the fact that he was stuck with the check. Burt seemed troubled as he told Loretta the story. His brow was constantly

47

wrinkled and he frowned at inappropriate times. After he repeated the story about the patient and the trochanter, Loretta interrupted him to say how terrible she thought it was for that patient.

Burt groaned. It took a little time to convince her that the trochanteric tale was a complete fabrication. She accepted that reluctantly.

"But it is a good example of what could happen," she said. "And it has a good moral to it."

"What is the moral?" Burt asked, wondering about Foxy-loxy.

"Stay away from doctors!" Loretta said.

"That is no moral to any story," Burt said without feeling hurt. He assumed she was kidding. "I'm sorry I told you that story. Almost as sorry that I told it to Charlie. It's the silliest story I ever heard."

"So why did you tell it? I don't think it's so silly." she confessed.

"When he said, 'Why do doctors *commit* malpractice?' I thought that was a silly question and deserved a silly answer! A doctor doesn't wake up one morning and say to himself, 'This is a good day to *commit* malpractice.' And the point of the story is that if they did, if they actually planned it, they probably could get away with murder."

Burt stopped suddenly and brought himself to his full sitting height very sharply.

48

Loretta also looked surprised with her eyes wide open.

"I didn't mean that," Burt sighed, sagging into the back of the chair.

"What did you mean?" Loretta asked softly.

"I don't know." he said shaking his head slowly. "Maybe I'm just upset because of the way Charlie just threw it at me. I thought he was joking. You know, patients are dying to get into the hospital, ha-ha. A bad joke—but he was very serious. I just can't believe that anyone, much less a doctor, would go to such lengths to cover up a mistake."

"Maybe he was just teasing you," Loretta comforted. "He was baiting you, that's all."

"Maybe," Burt said thoughtfully.

"Of course he was," she said smiling in hope it would cheer him up. "Look how upset you're getting. It was just a practical joke from one old friend to another. Why else would he do it?"

"Loretta, he's not an old friend. I hardly know him. Even way back in the eighth grade, I hardly knew him. He was a loner and a jerk. I don't know why he did it but there are two good reasons for me to be upset.

"In the first place, if it's not true, then he should never have spoken to me that way. There are too many people taking pot shots at doctors and he is in a good position to take pot shots.

"In the second place, if he does have something to go on. . . , I can't conceive of the second place. I'm in that hospital almost every day of the year. There's no way he could be right."

FIVE

Burt didn't lose any sleep over it. "It" was Charlie Dresden and his groping accusations. But it was there when he awoke the next morning. He didn't think about it actively. It just popped up in the back of his mind occasionally.

Aside from Loretta, there was no one to whom he could confide this type of speculation. Not even Nathan Simon, who knew Charlie Dresden.

He started rounds in the ICU a little after eight, the usual time for him to make an appearance there whether he had a patient or not. There was always a fresh pot of coffee at that time. He also had to admit that he liked to see Joan Chimento "swish." That was Loretta's word. It was inadequate to encompass Joan.

She had a bright light burning within her that overwhelmed the dark perplexities of daily life. It was a happy beacon that signaled she was there to do the work she liked. It flashed "yes," but it was a mistake to assume too much.

The package all this came in was bright and beautiful. Whatever part was picked, the eyes, the lips, the body, most any man would wish it was he who brought the "yes" to her eyes. But it was her reaction to living rather than to any man that made her look this way.

Perhaps out of modesty and because of Loretta, Burt saw an energetic professional nurse who always had the answers he needed. If the attraction was anything more, he never mentioned it.

The coffee pot was in the small conference room that was part of the ICU. The wall was gray tile up to four feet from the floor; the rest was standard plaster painted light blue. At one end, there was a small kitchen with compact components: sink, refrigerator and stove. Burt was leaning against the sink sipping his coffee when Joan walked in.

"Good morning," she smiled brightly and Burt could feel the electricity generating from within her. It wasn't only the coffee that perked him up in the morning.

At times he could act like a grizzly bear. He would brood and his jowly face would sag sternly. Sometimes he was just too tired to get the happy muscles working. This morning he was too deep in thought to match her brightness.

"Pardon me! I'll come back after you've had your coffee," she teased him carefully for not responding to her, bringing a smile to his face immediately. He looked and felt better.

"Ah, there's life in that body after all," she said. "Have you seen Mrs. Bentley yet?" she asked quickly getting down to business. "JoAnn is in with her now," she said referring to one of the staff nurses. "She's doing very well. She lost ten pounds since she was admitted. Her urine output was over four thousand cc's," she referred to a clipboard she carried with her

"Very good," Burt said. "How's her respiration?"

"About twenty to twenty-four a minute. She's comfortable now. No dyspnea and she pulled off the nasal oxygen and refused to let us put it back on."

"Did she pull out her IV?" Burt said implying that he expected she would.

"No," Joan chuckled a little. "She kept warning all the nurses to be very careful about it because Dr. Josephson wanted it there for a few more days. We changed the dressing around it and adjusted the armboard. She thinks you're some kind of god. All she could say was, 'Dr. Josephson put that in himself' whenever anyone went near it."

"Did Klein see her yet?" he asked referring to the consulting cardiologist.

"Yes he did. He left a note agreeing with everything you're doing and doesn't want to follow her. Do you think she can be transferred today?"

"Just what I was thinking myself," Burt said. "The mortality in this unit makes it dangerous for her to stay any longer."

"I like that," Joan said with good natured indignation.

Mortality in the unit was something to be expected. The sickest patients with life-threatening conditions were placed here for intensive care, so naturally the mortality rate was higher than anywhere in the hospital. When a patient's condition worsened elsewhere in the hospital he was immediately transferred to the ICU.

"I wish she could stay here until she's

ready to be discharged," Joan went on. "It would be good for my nurses to see someone fully recover. It's so much easier for them to burn out here than on the other floors."

"Burn out" was quickly becoming a common term among the service professions. Teachers, social workers and nurses were burning out after a few years on the job. The spark within was extinguished by repeated failure. No matter how hard they worked, it no longer seemed to make a difference.

The idiom was new but the phenomenon had existed since antiquity. ". . . one fire burns out another's burning;/one pain is less'ned by another's anguish;" Shakespeare wrote. For the nurses in the ICU, the flame within could not withstand the anguish without rekindling.

It was unlike Burt to be critical of nurses, especially those in the ICU—and Joan Chimento in particular, but this morning his mind was filled with thoughts of death put there by Charlie Dresden.

"Do you keep any records, something like the log they keep in the operating room?" Burt inquired, more concerned with his own phantoms than Joan's feelings. She swallowed a little of her pride and the flame burned less bright.

"There's no permanent log," she said. "There is the card index for each patient but that's part of the hospital record."

"So there is no way to look back and see how well you've been doing." Burt wondered out loud. Unfortunately, Joan heard an unintended emphasis on "you" and it showed in her face by the sad drooping of her eyes. She was wounded by the unaccustomed criticism from Burt.

"Why are you asking these questions?" she suppressed her annoyance. "No one ever asked us to keep a log of patients."

"It's not a bad idea," Burt suggested, modifying his tone as he recognized he was unintentionally challenging Joan. "You can go into the O.R. and find a list of patients and operations for the last five years or longer if you go the the storeroom."

"What good does that do?" she asked derisively.

"There's a monthly summary of all the cases done. It just keeps tabs on things. If a problem arises, it's easy to go back and look over the statistics to see if there is any pattern or continuing problem," he explained, his tone increasingly neutral. Joan took it personally, anyway.

"We keep a book of problem cases," she said defensively, "so we can bring them up and discuss them at our conferences."

"May I see it?" he asked.

Joan stepped out of the room. A few minutes later, she returned with a worn composition book of the kind used in grade school. It contained some hastily scribbled notes by various nurses going back about two years. A few notes were carefully written, most of these by Joan Chimento.

Burt read a few of these notes. It was not what he had in mind. No patients were mentioned specifically. The notes dealt with equipment and procedure problems. The oxygen outlet in one room was stiff and didn't take a plug easily. Where was the back-up oxygen for that room? Another was a reminder that a review of techniques for endotracheal suction was needed. And so it went. A series of reminders to make the Unit work more smoothly. There was even a note suggesting the coffee pot needed replacement.

"It doesn't really matter," Burt said handing the book back to Joan. "It was just a thought I woke up with this morning."

He dropped the issue but the depression clung to Joan. She followed him to Mrs. Bentley and watched without comment as he examined her. Mrs. Bentley was very happy to hear she would be transferred that day. One thing tempered her pleasure. She couldn't understand why Joan seemed so sullen. Only a half hour earlier, she was the one who enthusiastically promised her Dr. Josephson would agree to the transfer.

If Burt wanted to believe Charlie, the Intensive Care Unit was a good place to look.

It was an area of concentrated mortality. There were about three thousand patients admitted each year to the hospital. He had no definite idea how many died. Perhaps a hundred and fifty to two hundred. The pathologist did about fifteen to twenty autopsies a year. The autopsy rate was about ten to fifteen percent, so it could be over two hundred deaths a year.

"I'm going to miss you, Joanie," the prim Mrs. Bentley said sadly. "I hope they're all as nice as you are."

She had never been in a hospital before and mistrusted the idea of other people taking care of her. Joan and her staff had altered that notion a bit but Mrs. Bentley still suspected they were exceptional.

"They are very nice," Joan assured her, "and I'll be up to see you."

Joan really meant it and gave her a hug to seal the bargain. She would visit her for her own sake as well as Mrs. Bentley's. Joan wanted to see her completely well and back on her feet.

"Am I going to see you any more?" Mrs. Bentley turned to Burt who had been standing by, lost in his own thoughts. She was not one of his regular patients. He had been the physician on call for patients who came to the hospital without a doctor of their own. Just as she disliked hospitals, she had no use for doctors until she was near death. She had grudgingly allowed him to treat her in the belief that it didn't make any difference. She had accepted the end of her long life with equanimity.

"Every day until you leave the hospital," Burt said. "And I'll also see you from time to time after that."

"So you want to be my doctor," she said in a questioning but pleasant tone.

"That's entirely up to you, Mrs. Bentley," he said formally. "If not me, certainly someone else so this kind of thing that brought you here can be avoided."

He was a little annoyed with her. Burt had a very busy practice without her, but he sensed she would not seek another physician. For her sake, he accepted her stiff presumption of independence.

"You'll do," she replied and turned to Joan. "At least with a belly like his, he won't be lecturing me about diets and whatnot."

Joan laughed but Burt didn't think it was funny. He walked out.

Joan assured Mrs. Bentley that it was okay but she didn't need to. Mrs. Bentley meant exactly what she said.

An austere Dr. Nathan Simon walked into the ICU. He wore a white cotton coat that reached to his knees. Depending upon who wore it, the coat was either a lab coat or a professorial coat. In medical school, first- and second-year students wore this type of coat in the laboratory. They were required to wear short white coats in the third and fourth years and on through internship and residency. Instructors up through professors wore long white coats, so that even at a distance, rank was discernible in the hospital.

Nathan looked professorial in the neatly pressed white coat over a white shirt and dark tie. He also looked ghostly with his full head of white hair and pallid complexion. Tall, thin and unsmiling, he appeared quite different from the way Burt knew him: he projected such warmth at the bedside that he quickly gained the confidence of the patient. For this reason, in addition to his knowledge, he was frequently used as a consultant by many other physicians.

"How was New York?" he inquired as Burt walked up to him behind the nurse's desk. There was a remote bank of oscilloscopes screening the patients around the room, a silent green line breaking into repetitive hills and valleys in response to the electrical activity of the patients' heartbeats.

"New York was like New York," Burt shrugged. "Expensive and crowded."

Joan had left him to go on to other patients and to help her staff with routine care. There were four other nurses working there. They moved about from the patients to the desk and to the medicine cabinet, ignoring the two doctors.

"Where'd you have lunch?" Nathan asked, more interested in New York than in Charlie.

"A very nice place! And I wanted to tell you that I ordered clams in garlic sauce and fish with a creamy mustard sauce," Burt carefully sidestepped the fact that he didn't eat much of it. "I had no ill effects from it, either, so you were wrong about my gallbladder."

"I shall ignore that last remark," Nathan said raising his eyebrows. "You're not one of my patients, only my best friend and that's very shaky." The cold blast directed toward Burt was not taken seriously by either.

"We should have a monthly mortality conference," Burt changed the subject.

"Why?"

"We had them at the County when we were interns. They were very interesting, don't you think?"

"Yes, but it was a much more active place," Nathan objected. "There were a great many more autopsies and that's all that was discussed. I think we should get more autopsies. Otherwise, the discussions become just another clinical conference."

"I agree there were a lot of surprises in the autopsy but with all the lab tests, CAT scans and the rest, there's still a lot to discuss," Burt said.

"What do you mean by surprises?"

Nathan asked.

"The unexpected," Burt said almost argumentatively, "which you know happens quite frequently. A coronary that turns out to be a pulmonary embolus and vice-versa. A gallstone that turns out to be a cancer instead."

"So what good is a mortality conference without an autopsy?" Nathan felt he had proven his point. "It remains purely speculative without it except when it's obvious and then it's hardly worth discussing."

"There should still be some sort of mortality conference if only to keep track of the statistics, don't you think?" Burt persevered, if meekly.

"I don't know. Let me think about it." Nathan meant he didn't think it was a good idea at all. "How about what's his name, Charlie—what's his name?"

"He's a very strange guy," Burt picked up Bentley's hospital record, signaling that he was going back to work. "We talked about old times, had a few laughs. His work is very interesting."

"He's a reporter," Nathan said curiously, "Why did he decide to call you after all these years?"

"No special reason. Maybe he was lonely," Burt said looking away from Nathan. "There's nothing unusual about having lunch with an old childhood friend once in a while. Do you have any?''

Nathan Simon ignored Burt's uncharacteristic backbiting and walked off without another word. Burt felt foolish about lying to Nathan about the luncheon and about trying to get even for his remark about the shakiness of their friendship.

He disliked keeping secrets but now found that telling one would be even more distasteful. It made him scowl and insult Nathan. He was afraid Nathan would take him for a fool if he repeated his conversation with Charlie. He couldn't bring himself to make Charlie sound like a fool because there was an element in his tone, perhaps it was in his eyes, that made Burt take him seriously. Burt was sure Charlie was no fool.

SIX

Mrs. Bentley was discharged from the hospital the following week. She was more cordial toward her doctor now that she felt she had several more good years left to her if she followed his advice.

With Burt's encouragement, Loretta had decided to go back to work. In her new white uniform, she looked younger and lovelier than he remembered. When he saw her at a distance, in the hospital hallway he was attracted by her familiarity without fully recognizing her. For a moment, he was going to turn his back to the pretty new nurse who was trying to get his attention.

After the first day, he got used to seeing her in uniform. She was taking the in-service orientation program with a small group of new nurses. Most everyone knew she was Dr. Josephson's wife but it made very little difference. Only on that first day did she go out of her way to attract his attention. After that it was a formal greeting which he returned and then ignored her.

A day or two later, she was with a group of new nurses listening to an in-service instructor lecturing in the hallway. Burt and another physician were walking past them. It was obvious that he was just going to go by without even nodding to her, so as he passed, she threw him a loud kiss with a sucking sound that got his and his friend's attention. Burt pretended not to notice and kept on walking.

"Who was that?" asked Dr Brandon, a young, recent addition to the staff. "Was it for me or you? She was—"

"Don't say any more," Burt interrupted him. "I'll ask her when I get home tonight."

The medical records department was able to answer some of his questions. It was quite easy to get a list of patients who had died in the hospital in the past year. It was on the computer which printed out a list of names, dates, diagnoses and doctors. Three hundred and eighty-seven people had died in the hospital in the last year, and Burt's quick perusal of the list was uninspiring.

There was nothing to pique his curiosity even after Charlie had stung him. The list looked quite innocent and natural. It seems redundant to say they all died of fatal diseases, but a list such as this could only provide such limited information. Burt's curiosity was still unsatisfied because there was no established formula that could decipher the death list in the hospital. It was too easy to make any death there seem natural.

Charlie had said he would call if he learned something more concrete but Burt could see why he would have trouble. Not that he believed Charlie; it was just probable that Charlie had nothing to go on because nothing like murder had happened here. Burt decided not to embarrass himself by asking too many questions or doing a lot of fruitless research. The problem was an itch that would go away if ignored. It almost worked that way but Charlie called two days later.

"What have you found out for me?" Charlie asked.

"There's nothing to find out, Charlie,"

Burt said smugly. "I reviewed the deaths here at the hospital in the last twelve months. There is nothing unusual about any of them."

"You actually reviewed the charts of three hundred and eighty-seven patients?" Charlie asked dubiously.

Burt's smugness was shattered, as if Charlie had been spying on him and he had been caught in a lie.

"You need to compare those charts with the minutes of the Tissue Committee," Charlie said enthusiastically.

"Wait a minute," Burt protested. "How do you know there were three hundred and eighty-seven deaths? And the Tissue Committee meetings are no business of yours. Those minutes are confidential!"

"Stop it," Charlie said softly. He didn't want to antagonize Burt but at the same time he felt very sure of himself. "It's a public hospital and what goes on there is public information."

"No way, buddy," Burt said holding his ground. "The minutes reflect the private thoughts of the people involved. And furthermore, there is also a lot of personal stuff about the patients discussed. So you have no right to see them."

"Bullshit!" Charlie retorted. "No one gives a damn if Mrs. Jones had her gallbladder out or whatever. The official minutes are pure and simple whitewash. It's

67

nothing more than a script of play acting which no one bothers to read. The only reason to hide those records is their insipidity.''

"There's a lot more to it than that," Burt insisted, although he had never read the minutes of any surgical meeting. It wasn't his area of practice. "The Committee isn't the Inquisition. Besides, if it seems bland to you it's because there is nothing to get excited about. If someone steps out of line, a few well-placed words can straighten it out quickly.''

"Politics as usual only breeds conformity," Charlie said.

"Did you get that from a fortune cookie?" Burt said sarcastically.

"Very good. But it's not very funny," Charlie said so Burt could almost feel him gritting his teeth. "The killer is using that conformity to cover his tracks.''

Burt winced when he heard the word "killer." The first time, at the restaurant, it had bounced off him because he didn't take it too seriously. Now he felt he was in a verbal duel with a tough Charlie Dresden he never knew.

"Charlie, I resent your attitude," he said nervously trying to control his temper, "especially the way you talk about a killer." He was aware of the iciness his voice carried. "If you can't give me any evidence then let's forget the whole thing.''

Burt rearranged his desk top moving a few patients' records around, shuffling some correspondence he had been working on when Charlie called. There were one or two patients in his waiting room by now. He disliked keeping them there while it seemed he was just wasting his time with Charlie. The next move was up to Charlie who was thinking about it while the phone remained silent.

"Okay," Charlie conceded, "I'll show you the evidence but you must keep it confidential. No matter what you think, I don't want to discuss it with anyone else."

"That doesn't make sense," Burt said feeling confident. "If your evidence is so hot, why not use it before someone gets hurt again?"

"I'll be over about five-thirty," he insisted. "As you'll see, it's not that kind of evidence. If you act prematurely, he'll be scared off and—"

"You know who it is!" Burt said sharply.

"Just give me a chance to tell you what I know. I'll see you later. So long," he said, and hung up before Burt could press the issue.

Burt walked out to his nurse's desk down the long corridor from his consulting room. The office was conservatively decorated in browns and beiges. It was well-organized and efficient so he could go easily from room to room. A small laboratory was next to his waiting room where he or his nurse could do simple blood tests and urinalysis.

His nurse of the past ten years was Karen Eberle. She was a very small woman, no more than four foot ten in her stocking feet. Even with the three-inch heels she always wore, she just reached to Burt Josephson's chest. The contrast made her seem doll-like.

She wasn't pretty. Her nose and lips were a trifle too big for her face but she made herself look attractive with the right makeup. She was slim with a nicely rounded figure which, if small, was anything but child-like. She was also aggressive, as if to make up for her small size.

"How many do we have waiting?" Burt asked.

"It's about time!" she chastized him. "There are five out there," she stage-whispered, pointing to the glass window that separated her from the waiting room. "And Mrs. Dimarzio has been waiting in room three since you got on the phone."

He never liked the mother-hen attitude Karen displayed privately toward him when he was delinquent. At first, he thought she was cute and let her get away with it because of her size. It was no help for him to reason with her because she was usually right. Bullying was out of the question. It was obvious that she was too good to fire.

He was already frowning because of Charlie and falling behind in his office schedule did nothing to lift his spirits. Mrs. Dimarzio was close to eighty years old. She was so much like Eberle that she could have been her grandmother. She was about her height, but weighed close to two hundred pounds. Everything hurt but except for arthritis, there was nothing much wrong with her. And it wouldn't hurt if she lost about a hundred pounds and took the weight off her feet.

"Do you know how long I've been sitting here freezing to death in this paper dress?" she attacked Dr. Josephson as soon as he entered the examining room.

Burt took a deep breath that hunched up his shoulders as he buttoned the white lab coat up the front. Mrs. Dimarzio sat on the front end of the examining table with her stumpy legs dangling below. Her feet couldn't reach even the step at the bottom.

Burt walked around to examine the ankles which were obviously swollen. He pressed one with his finger and an indentation remained, indicating fluid retention.

"Ouch!" she screamed. "That hurts. What are doing there?'"

"What have you been eating?" he said unsympathetically, knowing she never kept to any semblance of a correct diet. The swelling was much greater than usual, implying she had recently consumed too much salt.

"Never mind what I've been eating," she said, dismissing his inquiry with a wave of her arm. Folds of fat hung like drapes from her upper arm. "What have *you* been eating? Look at that stomach of yours!"

Burt stood a little taller and sucked it in. His eyes narrowed and his lips pursed as he prepared to approach her again.

"We're not here for my health, Mrs. Dimarzio," he said. "I'm not eighty years old so I can handle the weight a little better than you can. The way that ankle is swollen, you've had too much salt. It's not how much you eat but how much salt your heart can stand. You've had too much salt lately."

"I never have salt." She was offended by the accusation. "That's not why I'm here, anyway. Forget about my foot. Look at this."

She threw open the paper gown and lifted up an enormous left breast which hung down to the top of her hip bone. The skin crease was red and excoriated with areas of white cracking and peeling.

"Right there, right over my heart. Every time I touch it, it hurts terribly. I'm sure it's my heart," she said simulating her pain for the doctor.

"How can you touch it?" Burt asked. "It takes your two hands just to lift the breast."

"Shut up!" she blasted, dropping the breast, obviously embarrassed that he noticed. "I breast fed all my ten kids. What do you expect? When I do this," she let her right hand disappear under the left breast, "it hurts when I press here."

"It's just a rash because no air gets in there," he tried for a simple explanation to satisfy her. "I'll give you a salve. Keep it as dry as possible."

"How do you know it's not my heart?" she insisted. "It's right over my heart, isn't it?"

"It's not your heart giving you the pain."

"Is my heart okay?"

"No, it's not. Look at how your legs are swollen."

"What has that got to do with my heart up here? Shouldn't you take an x-ray?"

"You had an x-ray two months ago."

"How was it?"

"I told you your heart is a little bit enlarged but it could just be fat around the heart."

"What are you gonna do for this pain?"

"Use this salve as directed," he said, writing a prescription, "and I'll have to give you a diuretic. Stick to the diet I gave you last time."

"Oh, you and your diets. Someone oughta give you one."

Burt conceded by letting her have the last

word. He stepped into the hallway and was about to ask Karen about the next patient. He thought he should call Loretta to let her know he might be home late tonight.

"Will you get my wife on the phone?" he asked.

"She's not home," Karen sounded pleased.

"How do you know?" he looked surprised.

"She's working, remember?"

"Well, try her later. She should be home by four," he said quite irritably.

He was annoyed that Karen remembered and he forgot. Charlie Dresden irritated him and he felt annoyed at himself for not spending more time with Mrs. Dimarzio. She always did what she wanted, anyway.

He decided that it wasn't his day to be very convincing about anything. He spent the next few hours seeing patients in a very low key. Nothing too serious came up and all the patients continued with more of what they had been doing before. At about three-thirty, Loretta called.

"I just called to say I'll be a little late for supper tonight," Burt said.

"No, I just called you," Loretta corrected him, "to tell you I won't be home for supper tonight. I have a chance to get the job in the ICU. I mean, I have it already but it requires going to Dr. Klein's weekly lectures on EKG interpretation for nurses."

"I can teach you anything Klein knows,"

Burt said, "while you're cooking supper, with extra credits for dessert."

"I'm sure you can, honey, but this is really part of the job. It sounds like such a good job I can hardly believe they're giving it to me."

"Why not? You deserve it and you're smart enough to handle it. What time will you be home? I can wait for you," Burt said eagerly.

"I won't be home until after nine. Why don't you grab a bite to eat at the hospital like you do when you go to a medical meeting?"

"After nine?" his voice rose incredulously. "Klein lectures until nine o'clock?"

"Well, no, some of the girls go out for a drink or something afterwards," she said apologetically but leaving no doubt she was going.

"Okay, hon, I'll see you later, then," he capitulated.

Charlie was late. Burt had seen his last patient and Karen went home, leaving him alone in the office. It was already past six. Ordinarily he would have left with or without Charlie showing up, but he had nowhere to go.

The silent, empty office assumed a clandestine ambiance while Burt waited alone for Charlie. It was a strange feeling to have in his own familiar office. The office was the same. It was the purposeless waiting that played on Burt. He thought Charlie was bluffing and he was just waiting to call his bluff.

Killer. Burt Josephson was waiting alone in his office for someone to come and tell him the name of an unsuspected killer. He looked around the walls at his diplomas. It was a strange word in these surroundings. He never dealt with killers.

Diseases were killers if one wanted to frighten someone into writing a check to a foundation of some other kind of fund-raising organization.

Charlie was supposed to tell him about someone he knew personally. It was clear that Charlie meant a physician, a colleague of Burt's, but there was no one Burt could even begin to think about in this way. He was wasting his time. Anyone Charlie named would be immediately rejected. There was no reason to suspect any deliberate deaths in the hospital.

Just before six-thirty, Charlie came, carrying a bulging eight-by-twelve manila envelope. If it contained evidence, there was a lot of it. He transferred the package from his right to his left hand as he reached over to shake Burt's hand. It looked as if he wouldn't let go of the package but he set it down right in front of Burt.

Charlie looked slightly frazzled. His dark blue tie hung down away from the open neck of his shirt. There were bags under his eyes that Burt had not noticed before. His suit was well cut and expensive but needed a pressing.

He hesitated and seemed puzzled about how to begin. Perhaps the way Burt retreated when the package was placed before him worried Charlie.

"You've got to promise me you won't discuss this with anyone," Charlie said apprehensively.

"I don't understand you," Burt said leaning forward and resting his hand on the package. He didn't want it to get away from him regardless of any promise he made to Charlie. "If this is any good, it should be exposed so the proper action can be taken before it can happen again."

Charlie sat at the edge of the chair shaking his head from side to side. He looked up at Burt sideways as if he didn't trust him at all.

"If you try to do anything with what we have here, you'll accomplish nothing. Maybe you'll scare him off." Charlie objected stabbing a finger in Burt's direction and annoyed at the prospect.

"What's wrong with that?" Burt said. "I think it's the most important thing to see that it doesn't happen again."

"No!" Charlie snapped and sat back in his chair. "He may have done this five, six, maybe ten times. I want him to get more than a wrist slapping by some medical board."

"Is there anything personal in this?" Burt asked softly as he saw the muscles around Charlie's eyes tighten.

"Does it have to be personal to rate your indignation?" Charlie replied, relaxing his shoulders and smiling through his thin lips.

Burt began to recognize the elements of a mental duel by the way Charlie smiled. Charlie was working on his curiosity and his fear that he knew something terrible about the hospital. But he seemed to be playing with Burt, teasing him, trying to make him want it badly. Burt decided to play.

"That's very clever," Burt said through hollow laughter as he pushed the package toward Charlie. "First you act like a head-hunter and then you settle for indignation."

"That's not what I said. I want you to be indignant enough to pursue the information I need. If you can't see it the way I do, I'd like you to forget the whole thing."

The smile had left Charlie's face and was replaced with concentrated seriousness. His voice was uncompromising.

"Even if I think you're wrong," Burt said, his voice rising. He was becoming agitated and it was clear that Charlie was much more used to this pig-in-the-poke bargaining than he.

"Even if your mind is set to crucify someone on innuendo or too little knowledge," Burt went on angrily. His indignation was rising, but in the wrong way as far as Charlie was concerned.

"No, Burt," Charlie said softly, relaxing and trying to establish a congenial atmosphere. "I won't try to talk you into anything. I want you to listen and to explain a few things to me. If you think I'm right then I want you to handle it my way. If you can show me I'm wrong, I'll forget the whole thing, I promise. I just don't want a half-baked confrontation."

"Before you go any further, spell out my options." Burt said cautiously.

"There are no options." Charlie smiled warmly. "I want you to evaluate the facts and the situation. Then you can tell me what to do next. There's nothing in this package which can convict anyone, but if you see it the way I do then I want to find out a lot more."

"And if I don't see it your way?" Burt probed.

"Prove it to me and I'll forget the whole thing," Charlie threw up his hands. "I told you that already but if it's in between, if you think something is wrong but all you want to do is call the Medical Society or have him kicked off the staff, then I want you to forget about it now."

"You don't think ruining a man's career, probably his whole life is punishment enough for a mistake?"

"I'm not talking about mistakes,"

Charlie leaned to grab the edge of the desk. "This was done on purpose to cover up a mistake. I don't want you to expose mistakes until we can prove it was murder!"

Charlie's eyes flashed and his eyebrows arched but he managed to speak calmly and forcefully enough to make Burt believe he couldn't say no without becoming an unwitting conspirator. Yet the proposition presented Burt with a dilemma. Unless Charlie had lost some of his marbles, the package on the desk contained damaging information against some member of the hospital staff. Dr. Josephson was obligated to bring this to the attention of the Executive Committee of the Hospital and possibly to the State Licensing Board.

Burt guessed that the package probably contained evidence of medical mishaps or even flagrant malpractice, but not evidence for murder. Charlie wanted help to develop evidence, and that would take some time. Meanwhile, someone else could be hurt and it was Burt's obligation as a physician to prevent it.

As Burt saw it, Charlie's games or conditions really didn't matter. He knew his own responsibilities depended upon the facts. He owed Charlie nothing.

Burt pulled the thick package across the desk and tore open the flap. Charlie didn't object; he sat back looking pleased because

Burt had committed himself. The package contained a sheaf of looseleaf papers constituting the hospital record of a patient named Hugo Demaris. The word "DIED" was stamped in big block letters on the front sheet, which also listed his vital statistics, diagnoses and surgery done. At the bottom of the page was the signature of Michael Bradley, M.D.

Burt shoved the stack of papers towards Charlie. His first thought was of how Charlie had obtained a copy of this hospital record, but that wasn't too important, after all. Anyone can get a copy of a hospital record by writing to the medical records department. It needs the patient's signature on a release form. Insurance companies do it all the time. If the patient is dead, the family can sign.

Burt accepted the fact that the medical record was not a classified document. It was just difficult to read and sometimes seemed to be written in code by the initiated.

"You're barking up the wrong tree, pal," Burt shook his head sadly. "I've known Mike Bradley for ten years. He's not—I can't even say it. It sounds so ridiculous. There's not even malpractice here."

Burt pulled the record to him and read the front sheet again. Charlie was steaming silently and from the distant look in his eyes, it seemed he wasn't listening to Burt.

The wheels inside his head were churning.

"You haven't even read the chart," Charlie said holding out his upturned palm in a way that was both pleading and accusing.

"Charlie, this is a very complicated case," Burt placed his hand on the stack of papers as if he were taking an oath. "There's a lot of surgery and many complications but it doesn't mean there was any malpractice. Mike Bradley is an excellent urologic surgeon. There's a good reason for everything that was done."

Burt could tell that much from the front sheet which listed six different diagnoses and three operations. Charlie's eyes focused sharply and then he burst out laughing. He slid down his chair and slapped his thigh exaggerating the levity far beyond his obvious reaction. Burt didn't find anything amusing. Perhaps Charlie had lost some of his marbles or maybe they were scrambled a bit.

"What's so funny?" Burt asked.

"You're treating him like a good ole boy," Charlie said seriously. "Anyway, that's what it sounded like to me except that I happen to agree with you. I didn't say anything about Bradley, did I? Let me tell you how I got into this."

Charlie's confident smile diffused some of the hostility between them. Burt began to realize how Charlie had orchestrated and revealed bits of information in a calculated way. He was ready for the finale to the overture.

"This isn't my kind of story," Charlie sighed, "but it really doesn't matter. War, politics or medicine. They are all the same. People are people."

War and politics were bedfellows. They were Charlie's usual beat but medicine was *Terra Incognita* for Charlie. That's why he needed Burt.

"Ed Martin and Bob Wishard are staff reporters who were working on a feature story about tuberculosis," Charlie went on, more at ease. "They interviewed a lot of families to see how they are affected by it. It's not that rare in the city but nothing like it used to be twenty or thirty years ago."

"I know," Burt said.

"The disease itself is not the social and epidemiological problem it used to be but it's still around. Their angle was the way the disease affected the whole family socially, even those members who were free of disease but still affected in other ways. In the Demaris family, there were two kids who had the disease. They were picked up by a screening skin test in school. As far as the family knew, only the two kids had tuberculosis. Marin and Wishard knew about the father but the family thinks he died of cancer."

Burt looked at the front sheet of the

hospital record and flipped through a few pages.

"This doesn't say anything about cancer," he looked at Charlie. "TB is the primary diagnosis. Then there's a list of complications—but nothing about cancer. Why did the family think he had cancer?"

"Dr. Beatty told them he died from cancer," Charlie said grimly.

"But didn't Bradley speak to the family?" Burt asked with more concern than needed. Even if Beatty was the family doctor, he was sure Bradley had had contact with the family.

"He said he did but the wife doesn't remember what he told her. She only knows what Beatty told her," Charlie raised an eyebrow when he mentioned Beatty.

"It's possible that she didn't want to believe Bradley because she felt guilty about the kids having tuberculosis," Burt searched for an explanation. "Beatty could have told her the truth or maybe he never told her the diagnosis. He could have left that up to Bradley. Mrs. Demaris might prefer the diagnosis of cancer. Did you speak to Dr. Beatty?"

"Ed Martin did and Beatty almost threw him out of the office. Luckily, of course," Charlie smiled, "Martin's an exwrestler, weighs about one-ninety and Beatty, I hear, is a little bit of a man. But he threatened to bash in Martin's face with a table lamp."

Burt discounted Charlie's version of the confrontation between Martin and Beatty. It showed on his face as a sort of sour expression that was both pained and incredulous.

Dr. Emery Beatty was in his sixties. Burt wasn't sure exactly how old he was but he had been there long before Burt and Nate Simon. He was well-established before the hospital grew and changed its character so dramatically. The changes altered Beatty's practice; he had been a general practitioner who did almost everything including a fairly large amount of surgery.

As the hospital grew, better trained younger surgeons appeared in the community. Beatty's surgical practice diminished and just about the time Burt came to Brady Memorial, he was listed only in the Department of Medicine with no surgical privileges.

"You don't look very impressed by Beatty's reaction," Charlie said annoyed with Burt's silence.

"I'm not," Burt said as blandly as possible. "I think your Mr. Martin was exaggerating. Beatty tends to be grumpy and has displayed a temper but I can't picture him threatening violence. You've been doing this sort of thing for a long time. You enjoy sticking needles into people."

"Wait a minute!" Charlie interrupted. "You're the doctor. You're the one who does things like that to people."

"So do you," Burt sounded tough, "but you do it for your own benefit. You know very well what I mean. You've built this whole thing up out of nothing by playing a little game with me. I don't want to play anymore."

"Why don't you call Dr. Beatty and ask him why he told Mrs. Demaris her husband died of cancer?" Charlie said so eagerly it bordered on pleading.

"Why should I?" Burt demanded. "Why should I play your games? You are making a false assumption. Mrs. Demaris was told the truth by Dr. Bradley. You said so yourself."

"Will you read that record very carefully for me?" Charlie demanded, annoyed.

"Why should I do it for you?" Burt tried to remain uncommitted.

"Because I saved your life!" Charlie insisted.

"You never saved my life!" Burt shot back.

"I would if I had to but you never took a chance at anything," Charlie smiled, his hands turned up in a gesture that was pleading but at the same time signified victory.

"Okay," Burt sighed, "I'll read it—but it won't help you."

SEVEN

Charlie Dresden was a moralist. So was Burt Josephson. Neither one could help himself. Their morality was pock-marked by cynicism and naivete, although not in the same proportions. Naivete matures into cynicism when dreams become nightmares. Burt and Charlie were two sides of the same coin, seeing the world from a different viewpoint.

Demaris died three months earlier, yet his case had never been presented to the staff at any conference as far as Burt knew. It looked very interesting and Burt thought it was just the sort of thing to be presented at a mortality conference. Perhaps it had been discussed in the Surgery meetings which Burt never attended.

There was no need for Charlie to beg or cajole Burt into reading this case history. After leading him this far, there was no way to keep Burt from the record. If Charlie hadn't left a copy, Burt would have gotten his own or the original from the hospital.

The front sheet of the record removed any mystery about the climax. It also gave Burt the advantage of hindsight as he read through it page by page. It afforded him the luxury of being critically correct and knowing this, he tempered his judgement.

It had been a mistake for Bradley to operate on Hugo Demaris but Charlie chose to ignore this. Everything Bradley did was out in the open. Hugo Demaris had been admitted to the hospital because of severe colicky pain in his right side. It appeared to be a routine case of a kidney stone passing down the ureter to the bladder. X-ray examinations confirmed the obstruction of the right kidney but a stone could not be seen nor was the right kidney visualized.

In severe obstruction of the kidney, the organ stops functioning. Nothing passes through the kidney, even the contrast fluid used to visualize the kidney. The point of obstruction was localized by cystoscopy and x-ray. It was the logical and necessary next step. Demaris was in considerable pain and running a low-grade fever.

Dr. Bradley had ordered light general anesthesia, and passed a thin telescope through the natural urinary passageway in the penis to reach the bladder. Handled carefully and delicately, the instrument can be passed painlessly if the patient is relaxed. Too often, though, his anxiety is so high that anesthesia is needed to get the patient to lie still long enough. In this case, Demaris was already in severe pain and the obstruction Bradley was looking for might need some manipulation.

The thin telescope, called a cystoscope, looks like a simple stainless steel rod. Inside this hollow tube, the optics are quite complicated and expensive. There are more than twenty lenses, tightly fitted in. Each lens is less than the diameter of the sheath, which must also carry a passageway for irrigating fluids to keep the bladder from collapsing on itself, and a bundle of glass fibers which carries the cold light. Each lens is no more than a few millimeters across, hand-polished and carefully aligned to transmit the image through the narrow tube with a minimum of distortion and minimum loss in light power.

Through this scope, Dr. Bradley could see a symmetrical pair of slit-like openings inside the bladder. These were the openings of the ureters, one from each kidney. The cystoscope allowed him to pass a fine hollow tube, a catheter with a diameter of less than two millimeters, into the ureter on the affected right side. It slid easily up the ureter toward the kidney. He advanced it through the cystoscope and watched it slither up the ureter until it reached an obstruction and resisted further passage. An x-ray film was taken of the abdomen with contrast fluid injected through the tiny catheter. Complete obstruction of the ureter was demonstrated about ten centimeters above the bladder. No contrast fluid reached the kidney.

The cause of the obstruction was still a mystery. Only one thing was certain: the obstruction had to be relieved. In almost any case except tuberculosis, the next step was surgical exploration. Statistically, the most likely cause was a stone lodged within the ureter. Even if the stone wasn't seen on x-ray, there are several types of stone which cannot be seen by that method.

It could have been a cancer originating in the ureter or one spread from an adjacent organ. It would have justified the immediate surgery and was more likely than tuberculosis. Tuberculosis was unlikely and it was the one diagnosis which required a preliminary course of medication before surgery.

Tuberculosis had been the scourge of the nineteenth century. It was ubiquitous, affecting the celebrated and the lowly alike, from Chopin to woodchoppers. "Consumption" robbed regardless of age or position. The tubercle bacillus was coughed up, spread by droplets, and inhaled by anyone near.

At the beginning of the nineteenth century, tuberculosis killed perhaps as many as one out of five people in the population. By the beginning of the twentieth century the rate dropped to one out of five hundred. The hundredfold decrease in the death rate occurred without any specific therapy for the disease.

The tubercle bacillus is a necessary component of the disease called tuberculosis, but its presence in the body is not sufficient to produce the disease. The host produces the sickness. The tubercle bacillus secretes no poisons, eats no flesh and reproduces more slowly than most bacteria. It is a passive organism that incites its host into rampages of self destruction.

A tubercular spot on the lung contains few tubercle bacilli, sometimes none, plus an immense outpouring of the body's white blood cells. These are white blood corpuscles gone mad, coalescing into multinucleated giants and destroying the body they were meant to protect. It was a company of knights foraging on the countryside and destroying the land they were called out to protect against invaders.

The bacilli do not erode blood vessels, but the body's own defenses cause the destruction, leading to an eruption of a bloody, caseating lung. It is a natural but extreme defense. Being natural doesn't make it a virtue; being extreme makes it a vice. Perhaps Charlie did have a point: war, politics and medicine, it's all the same.

There is no moral equivalent in nature. Bacilli have no morals or ethics, only chemistry. The biological analogy is always strained by a lack of true understanding. The law of the jungle is not kill or be killed, it is feed and be food. Nature can be manipulated but not set aside and ignored.

Dr. Bradley's error was nothing so profound. Tuberculosis of the lungs is the common form of this disease and even that is, fortunately, becoming rarer. Tuberculosis of the kidneys is even less common and always was. Bradley didn't think of it in time.

The surgery was needed but if Bradley had made the correct diagnosis, he first would have treated Demaris with antibiotics for at least three weeks. That would depend on the patient's condition. If the surgery couldn't wait, then he could have used a different approach, away from the point of obstruction.

The irony is that antibiotics often make the tubercular obstruction worse. The obstruction was in the ureter, which is a thin, worm-like muscular tube that propels the urine from the kidneys to the bladder. As the tubercular lesions heal, the smooth, supple muscles of the ureter are replaced with dense fibrous scar tissue. All the bacilli are dead but the ureter is useless. It's like taking a body count, declaring the battle won while the war is lost.

No politician could create greater ambiguity than nature does when tuberculosis is healed. In the massive fields of the lungs, a coin-sized tubercular lesion is isolated and surrounded by giant, multinucleated white blood cells. The body's reaction may be sufficient to eradicate the bacilli or perhaps they are killed with the help of two or three antibiotics. The coin-sized lesion which marks the destruction of the lung as well as the invaders is like an acre in the vast American prairie. The lung functions and the missing patch is unnoticed. On the other hand, a tubercular pimple in the ureter can shut down the kidney completely.

When Bradley explored the ureter, he opened it down its length in the area of obstruction. Above the obstruction, the ureter was ballooned out like a thick sausage that narrowed abruptly at the point of obstruction. Above the block, the stagnant urine was foul and purulent. The cause of obstruction was a walled-off abcess which he drained. At this time, the possibility of tuberculosis occurred to him, and he specifically requested special cultures for TB.

The ureter did not heal properly. Demaris improved as the infection was controlled with a combination of antibiotics and relief of obstruction. But the urine continued to drain from his side. After three weeks, it was clear that a fistula had developed between the ureter and the skin which would have to be repaired surgically. It was a complication due more to tuberculosis than the surgery.

Burt recalled some gossip about a patient with tuberculosis. The general discussion around the hospital was whether to keep the patient there or transfer him to the State Hospital for TB. Much of the staff, nurses and orderlies were concerned about contracting TB.

Demaris couldn't be transferred immediately after surgery. By the time he could be transferred, the tuberculosis was controlled and he was no longer spilling tubercle bacilli in his urine. He never had a positive TB culture from his lung sputum or his gastric washings. The final resolution was that he could be kept at Brady Memorial with proper precautions.

It was to be three or four months before the closure of the fistula was attempted.

That time span would insure a greater chance of success by allowing all the healing possible at the operative site. By that time all the scarring would have occurred so Bradley could see which was healthy tissue and which would have to be discarded. In the meantime, Demaris would wear a bag to collect the urine draining from his side.

He was almost ready to be discharged when he developed an acute myocardial infarction. He had no previous history of heart attacks or heart trouble. It seemed relatively mild. One night he complained of chest pain. A cardiogram showed some changes and he was immediately transferred to the ICU. The cardiac changes were mild with no apparent complications. Three days later he died.

Burt looked through every page of the hospital record. Emery Beatty had nothing to do with his hospital care. He was only mentioned once in the admitting history dictated by Dr. Bradley and that was merely an acknowledgement that the patient had been referred to him by Dr. Beatty.

It was a complicated case with a bad ending but there was nothing in it Burt could find that would be of any interest to Charlie. It took him more than an hour to read through the chart. Sometimes it was slow as he had to decipher the chicken scrawls that passed for Bradley's progress notes. It showed the doctor right on top of all the problems.

He spent more time than necessary looking at Joan Chimento's nurse's notes. They corroborated the care Demaris was getting as did the nurse's notes on the other two shifts.

There was something sensuous about her handwriting. Perhaps it was only the bold ink that made her notes stand out among all the others. The curved lines flowed neatly without spaces along the curves except where there ought to be spaces. Perhaps it was only loneliness that made the penmanship prurient.

There was nowhere Burt had to be. For the first time in longer than he could remember he was alone. There was no meeting or lecture to attend. No calls were expected because Nathan Simon was taking his calls tonight. It as an alternating arrangement he had with Simon. No patients, no meetings, no card game, no Loretta.

He never realized how much he had taken Loretta for granted. She was always there when he had nothing else to do. There were times when Loretta took precedence to other things in his life. Many, many times so long as they were planned in advance. They always worked around his schedule.

It felt strange, because Loretta had never left him alone. She had her life but if Burt got time off unexpectedly, she cancelled her plans without a second thought. For the first time, it seemed, something more important than Burt had arisen in her life. She had found something for herself. For the first time, Burt felt jealous.

It was a childish jealousy born from expecting her to be there when he wanted her. He was also guilty of seeing too much in Joan's handwriting. The sensuality he felt was the image of her in his mind rather than the lines on the paper.

If there was something peculiar about the way Demaris died, Joan Chimento may have noticed it without recording it in her notes. Maybe there was some detail filed away in her memory that could be recalled by careful questioning. For Charlie's sake, Burt rationalized, he should spend some time with Joan away from the hospital if possible. It would be easier to ferret out some lost detail in a more relaxed atmosphere. Burt was sure Charlie would do it that way.

He wanted to do it immediately. He wanted to call Joan and ask her to meet him somewhere to discuss Hugo Demaris. He couldn't do that. First, he had to find out if she remembered Demaris at all. Tonight, he just wanted to meet Joan but there was nothing he could do about that. Despite Charlie and after reading the case history carefully, there was nothing to get excited about. Except Joan!

EIGHT

Burt pretended to be asleep when Loretta came home a little before eleven o'clock. As soon as heard the automatic garage door open, he reached over and clicked off the light on the night-table.

At nine o'clock, he had been angry because he was alone. The medical journal seemed to be full of banalities or esoterica of no interest to him. By ten o'clock, he began to worry about her just as she so often did when he was later than expected. That was when he strayed off his diet if he could find someone to join him for coffee and cake or, even better, perhaps a banana split.

When he heard her coming in, he decided it was better not to talk about it until the next morning. Thinking he was asleep, she undressed in the bathroom and quietly slipped into bed.

The clock went off at five-thirty the next morning. Burt turned over and went on sleeping. Loretta jumped out of bed and was in the shower in a trice. When he opened his eyes an hour later, he saw Loretta in a sparkling white uniform topped off with a flat gauze cap on her head.

"Gotta go, honey," she bent over to kiss him.

"Where are you going?" he mumbled sleepily.

"To work," she said happily. "To work! I'll see you at the hospital."

"Wait a minute," he sat up, more alert. "It's only six-thirty. I thought you were still getting oriented at the hospital."

"I am! Right in the pressure cooker," she said. "I start working in the ICU today. Under supervision, of course. That's why I'm on days for now. Next week, I'll be on my own, working three to eleven. See ya later," she waved hurriedly as she left.

"Three to eleven!" Burt groaned loudly, but it was too late for Loretta to hear.

The prospect of "three to eleven" was troublesome. It meant Loretta would not be home when Burt got home at night. When she was through with work and home around midnight, Burt would be asleep.

He was still trying to work it out as he applied a thick layer of foamy shave cream to his round, heavily stubbled face. His eyes were still sleepy; he blinked twice to stimulate his dull face.

He had broad shoulders and an athletic body rounded off by layers of fat which smoothly contoured the angles like thick icing on a cake.

"Loretta, you're making a big mistake," he said to the mirror. "You're taking on too much for yourself. You'll miss playing tennis and bridge, not to mention Hadassah."

He bent his head to one side and stretched out his chin so he could scrape away the beard. When he relaxed, the double fold returned neatly into place. He stretched the clean chin, holding it there with wishful admiration but it wouldn't stay that way on its own. He relaxed.

"It's my fault. I neglect her. I could use her in the office. But she would never let me fire Karen Eberle, that little imp. The hours are better and the fringe benefits are excellent. She already has the fringe benefits. What's so great about working in the ICU?"

"Where did I go wrong? Loretta doesn't need the money. Kuchen, kinder and kirche! Who said that? I better not repeat that in front of her.

"Arnold and Roger, what will they think? They don't even bring home their dirty laundry anymore. Aren't grown sons supposed to do that for their mother? Arnold's living with some girl in Boston. What's her name? Probably does his laundry, but what about Roger? He's still a baby. Some baby, he's almost twenty-three. I was married already.

"He's not seeing anyone, I guess. Arnold's not serious either. Grandchildren! That's it. That could keep Loretta happy. No, I'm too young to be a grandfather. I'm not ready for it. We should have had more children. That would have kept her from running off.

"She's not running off. She took a job at your hospital. I know, just when I was thinking about making my move on Joan Chimento. Who is she working for? Joan Chimento. Whoever is in charge of planning ought to be fired."

Burt settled for a double orange juice to sustain him. He rejected the coffee left for him by Loretta. With only two people, Loretta made two cups in the automatic drip coffee maker. She already had a cup and in the big pot, the rest didn't look like much. He pulled the plug but let the coffee sit in the pot.

For her first hour at the hospital, Loretta joined the other nurses to hear reports from the night shift. Mr. Fiore had pulled on his catheter, she heard, and some bleeding had started but it had stopped now. Bessie Cantor had required pain medication every three hours last night and now was completely zonked. All the Demerol had caught up with her. She was hard to waken but her vital signs were stable. And so on for each of the patients.

Joan Chimento assigned Loretta to prepare and distribute medications without supervision because of Loretta's previous experience. When Burt came into the ICU, Loretta was deep in concentration as she poured liquids, counted pills and drew up medications into syringes according to the doctor's orders. She was so intent on her task that no one could tell how anxious she felt about her responsibility.

With each order and each medication, her eyes flashed back and forth from the nurses' record to the doctors' order sheet then to the pharmacy ledger. Some of it was made easier by the packaging done in the pharmacy, but she still had to check on the

102

pharmacy because she was the one who handed the pills to the patient, not the pharmacist. The pharmacy forms made sure the right patient was billed. The nurses' notes made sure the right patient got the right medication.

Burt was impressed by her confident appearance. He was probably the only one who could detect the one sign of nervousness she displayed. It was peculiar to her; when she was very worried about what she was doing, she stood with her heels close together and her toes pointed outward. She didn't look up as he walked past her to the coffee/conference room of the ICU.

The conference room was deserted but the remnants of the early-morning report conference between the two shifts of nurses was quite evident. The table was strewn with empty and partially filled coffee cups. The ashtray was overflowing with cigarette butts and ashes. It looked more like the end of an all-night poker game than an early morning hospital conference.

Burt found a clean cup and filled it with coffee from the large percolator. He searched around the table for some sugar packets. There was no place to put his cup down in the mess. Someone had bumped the table, and there were several puddles of coffee lying there like mocha raindrops.

He placed his cup in the sink and

returned to the disaster area of the table. He quickly stacked all the styrofoam cups and deposited them in a trash barrel in the far corner. The plastic spoons and soggy sugar wrappings disappeared next. With a paper towel, he wiped the wet table clear just as Joan Chimento walked in. He straightened up immediately from his bent position over the table. He stood frozen with the brown-stained paper towels in his hands.

"Bravo!" Joan said clapping her hands over her head. "Don't stop now. You're almost finished."

"A little more applause, please. I work better to a live audience," he said as he finished wiping and ceremoniously dumped the wet towels in the trash.

"Bravissimo! Multi buono!" she said smiling and applauding a little less vigorously than before. "I'll fix your coffee this morning. You deserve it."

"I've got it right here," he lifted the cup from the sink and took it to the cleaned table. "Neatness counts, you know," he added snidely.

"I was just going to do that," she feigned apology. "Report took a little longer than usual. We're breaking in a new girl. Have you met her yet?"

"I think so. Is she the one who's so scared her knees are knocking together?" he said flatly and unconcerned.

"Stop it," Joan objected as she sat down with him and playfully slapped his arm. "She's really smart. As a nurse, I mean, which has nothing to do with you."

Burt was very pleased with Joan's assessment but he hid it carefully. He sipped his coffee and grimaced as if it were too hot so he could disguise his smile. He also sought to change to subject quickly.

"How long have you been here?" he asked.

"Here?" she blinked with surprise at the unexpected question. "Seven years, no this is my eighth year. Eight years," she said.

"And how long have you been married?" he asked.

"Eighty years. Just kidding. It only seems that long," she laughed. "Let's see, er—twenty years. I was a child bride."

"Twenty years?" Burt was genuinely surprised. "How old were you when you got married?"

"Eighteen, right out of high school," she said. "Four years later I was mother of two and then I quit."

"Quit what?"

"Quit having babies," she looked wide-eyed at him. "It was tough for a while. Every month was a traumatic episode for me until I got my tubes tied. I went to New York, had it done and came back the same day."

"Why'd you go to New York?" Burt

asked, puzzled.

"Because no one around here would do it without Jim's consent. That's my husband, Jim. So I went to New York and told the doctor I was divorced. He took the money and did it without a wink!"

"What did Jim say?" Burt looked astonished.

"What could he say? I told him before that two dollars paid for the license, not the body. Besides, he couldn't tell the difference. I didn't tell him for two years until I went back to school for nursing. He didn't want me to go. He argued, 'What if you get pregnant?' That's when I told him. He had a fit but he got over it.'

Burt sipped his coffee and wondered why she had opened up to him so casually. He had asked her some personal questions and he did know her for eight years but he just found out he didn't know much about her. He admired her more than ever.

It was also clear that she was now very proud of her bold strokes for independence which, perhaps, she hadn't been when she made them. It just seemed like the right time to let someone who she liked know what she was like. Or perhaps she was sensitive enough to give some support to Loretta without being patronizing.

Burt missed the point—or at least ducked it. He said nothing for a minute, until Joan made a move to leave. Her revelation gave him a feeling of intimacy he never reached with her before. He weighed his amorous inclination and decided to go with the clinical question instead.

"Do you recall a patient by the name of Demaris? He was here about three or four months ago," he asked.

"Oh, Hugo, poor Hugo!" Joan recollected sadly. "He was right there," she said pointing out the door to an isolated room in the corner of the ICU. Burt couldn't see where she was pointing but he knew the room. "He had the shiniest bald head I ever saw and he was so scared of dying."

"He was right," Burt said.

"I know," Joan sighed, distinctly more compassionate than Burt. "But there was more. He hated being isolated and felt suffocated with face mask he had to wear. It made him feel like a pariah."

"He was," Burt said. "Did you go into his room without a mask and gown?"

"I wanted to. It would have made him happy to feel like a normal human being again. Even if it was only one person who showed she wasn't afraid."

"But you didn't," Burt commented with the smug assumption that there are no such things as martyrs if they know better.

"No, I didn't," Joan was undisturbed by the division between her feelings and her action. Both were sincere because she did know better. "I've got a negative tuberculin skin test and I want to keep it that way. They say you have to take that awful medicine for a year if your skin test becomes positive even if your chest x-ray is negative."

"You're so smart," Burt smiled at her.

"What's your skin test, big shot?" Joan chided him.

"It's positive. I was converted in medical school with BCG vaccination."

"So you're protected against TB?" Joan wondered.

"No, it doesn't work. I'm just skin test positive, that's all."

"When was your last skin test?"

"Nineteen fifty-seven."

"You're awful, you know," Joan grinned. "You never do anything you're supposed to. What do you tell your patients?"

"Everything they have to know," he said, letting the question float. "How did Demaris die?"

"Very suddenly," Joan said as if she were stricken. "I left here at two o'clock for a Head Nurses meeting. I came back at three and he was dead. The girls said it happened like that," she said snapping her fingers. "The alarm went off and he was in V-fib. They zapped him but he wasn't breathing. Went right into V-fib again. There was no one to intubate him. Anesthesia came about fifteen minutes after the first alarm. Usually they get here sooner."

"No one else was around," Burt felt a social guilt because no one on the medical staff had responded quickly enough

"Well, Dr. Beatty was in to see him about fifteen minutes before but he was long gone when the alarm sounded."

"Was Beatty following him along with Bradley?" Burt probed, snapping to attention at this news.

"No, his name wasn't on the chart. When he had the heart attack, Bradley called in Klein to take care of him," Joan stated, looking puzzled.

"What's the matter?" Burt asked, noting her expression.

"I didn't know Dr. Beatty was his doctor or that he had been coming in to see him. Only that last time, after Hugo died, and Judy asked me if she should put it in the nurses' notes. I was surprised but since he never wrote any orders or progress notes it wasn't really a doctor's visit. Shouldn't he have asked Beatty to follow him if Beatty had referred the patient to him?"

"No, Beatty would have to get a consultation anyway," Burt said. "You were right. It was just a social visit."

Just a social visit, Burt repeated to himself. He had almost gagged on the words when he said them out loud. Charlie would have jumped on it, he was sure of that. But he wasn't sure it meant anything, even in the ugly framework Charlie had built.

Ventricular fibrillation was documented. It wasn't unique. That's why Demaris was in the unit. He was there to guard against such an eventuality. That's why patients with a recent coronary die suddenly. Instead of beating in a powerful, united beat, the muscle fibrils of the heart beat to an individual rhythm. In their cacophony of independent electrochemical beats, no useful work is done by the heart. The heart resembles a rubber ballon filled with water wobbling along a flat but bumpy road. Nothing is spilled; nothing is pumped out of the heart.

The muscle fibrils disarrayed, like an army with each soldier jitterbugging to his own tune, are snapped to attention with a jolt. It's not the shrill whistle of the first seargent but an overriding blast of four hundred volts of direct current shooting through the body. It's as if the parade grounds were lifted up and snapped like a tablecloth. When it came down smoothly, all the soldiers were back in place marching to "Stars and Stripes Forever."

It doesn't always work. It didn't work for Hugo Demaris. If the muscle is too badly damaged, it won't respond to any amount of electrical shock. It needs oxygen to respond and to sustain that response. Joan said he wasn't breathing during the resuscitation attempt. The mask and bag wasn't enough to push air into his lungs. He needed a tube but it was too late after they got one down his trachea. Was he not breathing before the ventricular fibrillation began? That could trigger it but no one saw him just before he went into V-fib.

Loretta Josephson came walking in very quickly. She had obviously run into a problem as she started to say, 'Joan—'' then halted in mid-sentence when she saw Burt.

"Excuse me," she said, "I didn't know you were having a conference."

She was deliberately formal and Burt noticed how tightly she kept her heels together and her toes pointed outward. He stared at her and said nothing, which only made her more nervous.

"Would you like to have a conference with Dr. Josephson?" Joan smiled broadly, hoping to ease the tension.

"No, I just came in to ask you about an order." she said, still tense. "Dr. Brisson ordered sodium bicarbonate and calcium chloride added to Mrs. Lester's IV. They are incompatible. What should I do?"

"The pharmacy will pick it up." Joan reassured her. "They mix all the solutions."

111

"But her IV will be out soon, the bottle hanging there is almost empty. Should I call Brisson and ask him to change the order?" Loretta asked worriedly. She avoided looking at Burt.

"C'mon, I'll call him," Joan said standing up. Loretta gave Burt a quick wink and a smile as she followed Joan.

Burt took in Loretta's performance with pleasure and pride. He assured himself things would work out for them. Anyway, he would try. He had also promised Charlie he would try to look at this case a little differently. Unintentionally, that difference had surfaced.

It started when Charlie brought this case to his attention. Even before that, the luncheon was designed to lay the groundwork for a different view of things. He knew what Charlie was doing but took none of it seriously until Joan mentioned that Dr. Emery Beatty was the last person to see Hugo Demaris alive.

Burt had read enough detective stories and had seen the procedures of TV cops to start thinking like one. Opportunity, means and motive immediately came to him as a different way of looking at things.

Opportunity was obvious. Dr. Beatty was alone with the patient. He knew the Unit's routine and he could come and go as he pleased. He had many chances.

As a physician, he had knowledge of a great many means which would go undetected and unsuspected as the inciting cause of death in a patient who had recently suffered a myocardial infarction.

In the ICU, every patient had an intravenous running into the vein. It was a necessary precaution so that any sudden change that required rapid action could be treated by direct injection through the open line. There were a host of substances that could be injected to produce the fatal arrhythmia. There were even some that would go unnoticed even if a thorough post-mortem toxicological examination were done.

Any foreign substance, even a rare one that acted in minute quantities, could eventually be detected. On the other hand, a common substance found in large quantities in the body can be made deadly under the right circumstances. Its presence has no significance as evidence for murder.

By physiological dimensions, there are huge quantities of potassium in the body's soft tissues. Next to sodium, it is the most common inorganic element in the body. There's more calcium if the bones are weighed but that is a secluded region.

Potassium is also segregated. There is almost a hundred times more potassium inside a living cell than there is outside in the tissue fluid and the circulating blood.

113

The reverse is true for sodium. Large quantities of sodium circulate in the blood and relatively small amounts inside the cell.

Potassium and sodium are charged particles which are the universal chemical carriers of bioelectricity. Segregated across the cell membrane at the cost of metabolic energy, these two particles move in and out of the blood and cells as the body functions, most notably along nerves and muscles. The rhythmic electrical changes detected by wires and recorded on the electrocardiogram is the electrical activity produced by the flux of sodium and potassium.

Numbers are important here. The amount of potassium per cubic centimeter of blood is critical for the normal electrical activity. Too much or too little in the blood drastically disturbs the rhythm of the heart.

A living, metabolizing cell membrane is needed to keep the balance of large amounts of potassium inside the cell and small amounts outside in the blood. When this small amount of potassium is increased to a concentration slightly less than twice the normal amount, it becomes toxic. The sodium-potassium balance is upset and the heart beats irregularly and suddenly stops. The rise in potassium can be produced by a direct intravenous injection of ten cc's of a potassium solution commonly found in every hospital.

At death, when metabolism stops, the cell membranes are functionless. The large amounts of potassium inside the cells reaches equilibrium with the concentration of potassium in the blood. The fatal injection of potassium is now a tiny fraction of the total body potassium, which after death is no longer segregated. Therefore, there is no way to detect the added potassium. It's like a bucket of water dumped in the ocean.

How does something essential for life become toxic? Concentrations. Try this question. Why is oxygen the most toxic substance in the world? Because a man placed in a room containing one part per billion concentration of oxygen in that room air will die.

Potassium wasn't the only thing a physician could use but it was the best. It was part of the body. It belonged there. It was non-toxic when used in the right amounts and deadly when used knowledgeably. After death, there was no way to tell how it had been used.

Potassium was perfect but even if another poison was used, if it were used, Burt conceded, what was the motive? Why would Beatty kill Demaris? Burt had only Charlie's suspicions to go on and he didn't trust them. Everything Charlie told him was slanted, designed to lead him along a preconceived path.

No one else connected with the case was

suspicious. Burt allowed that he didn't know that for sure. Just as he was careful not to voice his or Charlie's viewpoint, it was possible Joan Chimento felt the same way. Yet she did make a point to mention Beatty was present just before Demaris died.

Charlie had to know more than he was telling. Burt decided to call him before he started asking questions around the hospital. It was ten minutes to nine. By hospital standards, the morning was rapidly slipping away.

He called the newspaper and asked for Charlie Dresden. The switchboard put him through to Ed Martin.

"Martin," a nasal voice droned harshly through the phone.

"Is Charlie Dresden there?" Burt asked anxiously.

"Not in today," Martin said abruptly.

"Just tell him Dr. Josephson called," Burt was annoyed by the lack of interest at the other end.

There was a long pause in which Burt expected to hear a click followed by a dial tone. A vague recollection of Martin's name made him hold on. The same process of recognition worked on the other end.

"Can I help you, Dr. Josephson?" Ed Martin asked more pleasantly.

"I'm a friend of Charlie Dresden," Burt said cautiously.

"I know. Charlie and I have talked about you. Unfortunately, he doesn't usually get in here until the afternoon. Have you come up with anything on the Demaris case?" Martin asked eagerly.

"No, nothing at all." he said, not letting his nervousness creep into his voice. "I had a few questions for Charlie."

"Maybe I can answer them." Martin offered.

"Maybe you can," Burt assented, pleased with the offer. He had to think how to phrase the question. If it were Charlie, he would have laid it out flat even if he had to get angry. Martin was a source he wanted to play carefully.

"Dr. Beatty has covered his tracks completely," Burt talked if he believed everything Charlie had told him. "There's nothing to link him to Demaris except that he referred him to Bradley. There was no evidence in the chart that he had anything to do with him in the hospital."

"Nothing at all, huh?" Martin said thoughtfully. "So you think he never saw Demaris after he was admitted to Brady Hospital?"

Burt hated lying and hated being trapped by a lie even worse. He withheld Joan Chimento's comment about Beatty's visit, hoping to draw something substantial from Martin.

"Not that I know," Burt said firmly. It

wasn't the whole truth but he could always say he wasn't sure without corroboration of Joan's comments. "What made you think he did?"

"He did, Dr. Josephson," Martin insisted. "He did see him and he did kill him!"

Burt shuddered at the thought but also felt a flush of anger. He didn't like strangers who made accusations which seemed wild and unfounded. He didn't know Emery Beatty very well and had no feelings about him either way. Still, there was no reason for Beatty to be attacked this way as far as Burt could see.

"You have no right to say that!" he said angrily. "I want no part of a whispering campaign that could destroy a man's reputation. You can tell Charlie that if I find him or any of his gang snooping around the hospital, I'll blow the whistle on them. I mean to advise Dr. Beatty that someone is out to get him for reasons that make no sense to me at all!"

"Don't do that, Dr. Josephson," Martin pleaded. "He's killed at least ten patients and this is the closest we'll ever get to proving it."

"That's insane! You're insane!" Burt jumped at him through the phone. His face turned red. Then he took a deep breath and spoke calmly.

"Look, I don't know Emery Beatty very

well but he is a member of this staff. He is liked by his patients. He is a competent general practitioner.''

"I thought he was a surgeon.'' Martin interrupted.

"No, his surgical privileges were stopped here long ago,'' Burt sounded puzzled.

"He's still a surgeon over at Townbrook Hospital,'' Martin said, a silence followed. The reporter waited to hear how Burt would react.

"Why didn't Charlie tell me that?'' Burt asked.

"He said you'd find out for yourself, and in a way you did,'' Martin replied graciously. "He operated on Demaris at Townbrook.''

Burt was stuck. He didn't know what to say about Beatty's surgery. He couldn't quite believe it but knew it was possible.

"Is that it?'' Burt asked. "Or is there anything else about Dr. Beatty you'd like to tell me?''

"There is more but I'm not sure I should tell you.'' Martin said politely. "Charlie said you were a reasonable and thoughtful man but in a case like this, it is better if you could find things for yourself. We need your help, Dr. Josephson, but first you have to convince yourself that Beatty is dangerous.''

"You're right about one thing, Mr. Martin," Burt agreed—forcefully. "I'm not convinced."

"Give Charlie another chance," Martin said confidently. "I'll make sure he calls you this afternoon. In the meantime, just do what you've been doing and don't let anyone know why you're doing it."

After Burt hung up the wall phone in the ICU conference room, he sat down again at the table. Thinking about the conversation, he still felt manipulated. He was sure Beatty did surgery at Townbrook. It was a small, eighty-bed hospital about thirty miles west of Brady Memorial.

There was nothing in the chart to suggest that Beatty had operated on Demaris. Bradley only noted that the patient had been referred to him by Beatty. Burt was bothered by this. Bradley had the answer but Burt didn't know how to ask him without giving away Charlie's interest in the case.

As he pondered like a hulking bear with his broad shoulders hunched and his face made jowly by a frown, Loretta came in. She was headed for the cabinets behind him to get some equipment. She was surprised to find him still there.

"Is this how hard you usually work? No more sympathy from me when you get home," she laughed.

"Loretta, I've got to talk to you," he said in a heavy voice.

"I'm sorry Burt, I can't right now," she quickly went to the cabinets and found the round steel bowl she had come for.

"It won't do any good," she said quickly. "My mind is made up. I'm going to keep this job and you'll just have to get used to it."

"It's not the job," Burt started to say.

"I can't talk about it now," she interrupted him. "I'll see you tonight and we'll settle this whole thing," she said and strode out, carrying her bowl like a helmet at her side.

NINE

Loretta's belligerence confused Burt. Admittedly, he had been hoping she would give up the idea of working nights, but he didn't think he had been obvious about it. Perhaps she knew him well enough to know what he was feeling. More likely, he assumed, he talked in his sleep while she was getting dressed in the morning.

It was more urgent for him to share the problem of Emery Beatty with her. He was ready to capitulate to any reasonable arrangement for a few moments of her time and for her opinion on how he should act.

Instead, he felt burdened with two problems that were unfamiliar to him. A third one popped into view when he saw the coffee stain on the sleeve of his tan corduroy jacket. He rubbed it with a wet paper towel which left a broader, darker stain that he assumed would soon dry.

The hospital had settled into its morning routine. Breakfast was over. The trays had been cleared from the rooms and were tucked into the large mobile kitchen wagons. There was a nurse with a portable medicine cabinet down the hall. The pills and syringes were arranged in rows with each patient's name printed up front with his room number.

A few patients were taking a turn around the floor in their bathrobes and slippers; it was too early yet for visitors. The other nurses were in the rooms tending to those who could not take care of themselves. Some were young, recovering from surgery. A day or two more and they could be on their own. For some, the old and irreversibly ill, recovery was only a hope or dream.

Burt went over to the carousel rack containing the hospital charts for this floor. He spun the rack and pulled out, one at a time, the three charts of the patients he had here. Betty Flanagan, the charge nurse, came toward him from an adjacent room.

"You're late this morning," the tall, dark-haired nurse said.

She had a bent nose that was too big for her face. Her pale skin reminded Burt of stucco. Besides that, Burt didn't like her because she was very pushy and always second-guessed him. Maybe she was just curious but to Burt she always sounded critical.

"I'm not late!" Burt countered. "I'm self-employed. I get here when I want to."

"Pardon me," she said with exaggeration. "You're always here by eight-thirty. I told Mrs. Richter you would be here. She wants an enema now. I said you would order it."

"Well, just wait till I see her," Burt insisted. "It's bad medicine to do everything routinely."

"But you always order an enema after three days of milk of magnesia with no results," nurse Flanagan insisted.

"Well, maybe she has a bowel obstruction this morning," Burt retorted.

"Stop making so much noise," a familiar voice said softly from behind the other side of the chart rack. The carousel chart rack sat on a table and passed through a partition. On the other side was a small room with dictating equipment where the doctors did their paperwork. Nathan had been sitting there when Burt came over.

"Nate, I want to talk to you," placing the charts on the table. He started to go around to where Nathan was sitting.

"Wait a minute!" Betty Flanagan called after him. "What about Mrs. Richter?"

"Give her an enema," Burt continued walking.

"I already have, thank you," the nurse said, and turned away.

"Nate, I have to talk to you," Burt whispered. There were other people coming to the chart rack who could easily overhear them.

"Come with me," Burt said. The urgency and the seriousness in Burt's face left no room for Nate to argue. He followed Burt down the hall to the small room which served as kitchen for the floor. It was a narrow galley with one table against a wall and a sink, refrigerator and cabinets against the other wall.

Burt sat down while Nate stood stiffly waiting for him to speak. Nate wore his long white coat neatly buttoned and carefully pressed.

"What do you think about the Townbrook Hospital?" Burt asked.

"It's a pesthole," Nate shrugged.

He realized this was only the beginning of Burt's talk so he sat down opposite him. He leaned his elbows on the table, folded his hands and waited for Burt to get to the point.

"You're exaggerating," Burt said. He pulled one leg across the other knee and held his ankle to prevent it from slipping off. "What's the Surgery Department like over there?"

"You're not going to have your gallbladder done over there?" Nate asked in concern. His tone answered his own question without doubt.

"There's nothing wrong with my gallbladder," Burt insisted with obvious annoyance. "I asked you a simple question. Give me a simple answer."

"You never ask me a simple question," Nate corrected calmly. "It would be just like you to sneak off and have the surgery without telling anyone. Have it done here, for godsakes. What are you afraid of? So some nurse will see your pecker. Big deal!"

"Fuck you, Nate. There's nothing wrong with my gallbladder," Burt stamped his foot.

"Then why are you asking me about surgery at Townbrook?" Nate demanded as if it proved his theory. "I don't go over there and wouldn't recommend it to anyone."

"That's why I'm asking you," Burt said innocently. "You hear more things than I do."

"That's because I'm a better listener."

"Then shut up and listen for a minute," Burt said quickly. "A patient came to me for a second opinion. She's a patient of Dr. Beatty and he wants to strip her veins," Burt spun the story as he went along.

"Why should she come to you for a second opinion?" Nate was surprised. "You're not a surgeon. For that matter, neither is Beatty."

Nate's assertion embarrassed Burt. It looked like Martin had lied to him about Beatty's operating on Demaris. It also made Burt's story about the patient and her varicose veins improbable.

"That's what I thought," Burt faltered. Nate Simon didn't notice the flush around Burt's ears.

"But that doesn't stop him from operating," Nate added. "I would tell your patient to keep her varicose veins and if she still wants them stripped, she should definitely find someone else to do it."

"A stranger, someone you don't even know, you glibly divert from surgery. But me, your best friend, you're ready to stick a knife into," Burt mocked.

"I wouldn't even let you go to Beatty for surgery.,' Nate said knowing Burt would never think of using Beatty for a surgeon.

"Why not?" Burt asked. There was new life to Martin's accusation. Nate gave him a sour look.

"Despite everything you have ever done to me, I have a certain affection for you I can't explain," Nate said as he stood up to leave.

"Wait a minute," Burt waved him back to his seat. "Sit down and tell me what's wrong with Beatty. Why did he lose his surgical privileges here?"

"In the first place, he's not board certified. He's not even eligible. I'm not sure if he had any formal surgical training but he was doing surgery here at Brady before the new regime moved in," Nate stopped to think for a minute.

"Before you came here," he continued, then stopped again to think. "Did I get here two or three years before you?"

"Two years. What's the difference? Tell me about Beatty," Burt probed eagerly.

"Then it was over twenty years since his surgical privileges were revoked. When I got here he was still listed as a surgeon," Nate recalled. "It was that way until a new roster was printed.

"Why did they take his privileges away?" Burt asked.

"It was many things but they had to have something substantial before they could actually do it," Nate stood up again, sticking his hands in his pockets impatiently. "As a matter of fact, I think it was a case that involved vein stripping. I don't know how they got him but it caused quite a fight. I gotta go, Burt. My patients are waiting. If your gallbladder keeps acting up, go and see Alex Fineberg. He's an excellent surgeon."

"There's nothing wrong with my gallbladder, dammit!" Burt said, just a little bit angry.

Early in nineteen-sixty, the junior senator from Massachusetts won his first primary in an election which would carry him on to the Democratic National Convention, the White House, and ultimately, Dallas.

The day Kennedy won the election in New Hampshire was the day that Connie Belanger walked into Dr. Beatty's office complaining of a vague cramping sensation in her left leg.

It only ached occasionally, mostly when she had a difficult day with her two-year-son who cried a lot and insisted on being carried around. He had been difficult all along, much more difficult than her daughters who were now five and ten years old. He was happy and healthy but he was the baby.

She was thirty-two years old when the child was born. About six months before that, the ugly blue line popped out along the inside of her left thigh. By the time he was born, the vein looked like the Yazoo River from her groin to her knee. That was an exaggeration. No one but Connie and Dr. Beatty noticed it.

Connie and her young family had moved from the midwest to the north Jersey suburbs in nineteen fifty-five. She was pleased to find a doctor like Beatty who was a general practitioner. He would take care of the whole family, including any surgery, as he often reminded her. The family was healthy except for minor colds and sprains. He also encouraged her to get pregnant again.

"You're not getting any younger," he told her. "After thirty it gets much harder," he warned.

She passed her thirtieth birthday without getting pregnant. She carefully avoided pregnancy with the aid of her diaphragm but Dr. Beatty kept at her.

"Jennifer needs a baby sister or brother," he said as he wrote out a prescription for erythromycin and handed it to her.

"If Jenny only has a cold, does she really need this antibiotic?" Connie asked.

"Of course she does," Dr. Beatty assurred her. "Give some to her sister, too."

It didn't sound like good advice but Connie didn't contradict him. She had the prescription filled for Jenny but kept the medicine away from her sister Amy. She had read that common colds are not affected by antibiotics and certainly couldn't prevent them.

Of course, Jenny got better and as inevitably happens, her sister came down with the same symptoms a week later. Connie felt a little bit guilty about it even after Amy got better without antibiotics.

Her husband, Tom, didn't push as hard as Dr. Beatty did, but she knew Tom wanted to have a son very much. She forgot about her diaphragm for awhile. It was such a nuisance, anyway.

By her seventh month, Connie felt she was a big as a cow and hated the growing blue line running down her thigh. She cried bitterly about it one day in Beatty's office during a routine prenatal visit.

"No problem about that," Dr. Beatty said warmly. "After I deliver that beautiful baby boy for you and he's home and growing soundly, we'll just erase that blueline with a little nick right there," he pointed to a place high on her thigh.

She was feeling sorry for herself and Dr. Beatty's assurance was all she wanted. As it turned out, Tommy Jr. was well worth it. Soon after he was born, she quickly regained her firm, trim body. The blue vein receded but did not fade completely after two years. On days that seemed to stretch out and keep her on her feet, it stood out more prominently. She knew it was vanity and used the aching as an excuse to give in to Dr. Beatty's frequent reminders that he promised her he would remove it.

She was worried about Tommy, junior and senior, and the two girls. Her mother came to take care of things and to help after the surgery. Dr. Beatty assured her she would be back on her feet within two weeks. There was nothing to it.

The operating rooms at Brady Memorial Hospital still had the sparkle of newness about them. The new wing was actually more than a wing. It was three times the size of the old hospital. More properly, the old hospital was the wing. Brady Memorial was entering a brand new era.

In the surgical suite, the new stainless-steel-and-glass doors of the cabinets wiped clean and shined easily. The light blue pastel tiles were a relief from the glaring white of the old building. The disinfectant smell was banished.

Connie Belanger traveled in a twilight sleep, induced by Demerol and Seconal, beneath the soft white fluorescent lights in the hospital corridors. The new stretchers had hydraulic suspensions insuring a gentle, undisturbed ride to the operating room. She was unaware of her destination and free from anxiety.

In the operating room, she followed instructions as if sleepwalking. She extended her arm to the side and felt nothing as the intravenous needle pierced her skin to enter the fine vein in her forearm. A blood pressure cuff was wrapped around the other arm and the arm tucked inside a sheet at her side.

The anesthesiologist completed the preparations and was ready to begin. Bella Czerny, M.D. was about fifty years old but her face reflected a thousand years of horror when she was under stress. Each induction of anesthesia, for every anesthesiologist, is a period of great tension. Each tube and valve must be checked and double-checked. No plugs of forgotten dust or mucous can clog an oxygen line. The tanks must be full or nearly full so they don't run out at a critical moment.

Even the obvious must be handled with care. Is this the right patient in the right operating room? Is this the operation the patient consented to? Are there any special risks with this patient?

As she worked to fit each piece of the complex puzzle into place, agony flooded Bella's face. The pain was subconscious and associated with another time of stress indelibly etched into her soul. It was also tatooed in the form of a serial number on her right forearm.

She was practicing medicine when the Nazis marched her off to concentration camp in 1942. She survived but the body has a memory of its own. Stress, anxiety, fear, horror and pain lead to the secretion of hormones in different degrees as it teaches the body to react instinctively and prepare for the the next step.

With her preparations complete, Bella Czerny could relax for a moment. Relieved of stress, her face resumed its natural kindness. Her brown eyes became soft, warm and understanding as if her soul could reach out and soothe any pain and suffering. She knew every kind.

"Wo ist der chirurg?" Bella stood with her hands on her hips, ready to begin anesthesia. She was fluent in German but hated the language. She used it only sarcastically and contemptuously.

"Dr. Beatty is scrubbing at the sink," the circulating nurse answered.

The beep, beep, beep, of the EKG oscilloscope was the dominant sound in the room. Bella turned off the volume. The blue-green line passed silently across the screen with regular bursts of elevations and depressions. A nurse positioned the four-foot-wide spotlight over Connie's groin area. Show time!

The activity around her awakened Connie but she would remember nothing. Her eyes were open but her mind was elsewhere. Bella injected Pentathal through the intravenous line. Connie's eyelids sagged and her head flopped to the side like a straw doll's. Bella caught her gently around the ears. She placed a mask over Connie's face.

Connie's breathing inflated and deflated the black rubber bag hanging below Bella's anesthesia machine. Bella watched and gauged the rhythm and strength of the respirations. She adjusted the flow of oxygen and halothane. Connie's body relaxed more and more as Bella became tenser.

When her face twisted, the scar that ran from her lip to her chin disappeared. It was replaced by a burst of lines flowing symmetrically around the edges of her lips and seemed to cross the bridge of her nose.

Bella rapidly removed the mask from Connie's face. At hand was the gleaming laryngoscope. She held it by the heavy handle, containing batteries for the small bright light at the end of the curved blade extending almost at a right angle from the handle.

She held Connie's head back to extend the neck. With one hand, she opened Connie's mouth and held the tongue out over the lower teeth. With the other hand, she guided the laryngoscope blade back behind the tongue and down the larynx. Gentle back pressure on the scope pushed the larynx forward and opened the vocal cords. Releasing the lower jaw, which stayed open from the pressure of the scope, Bella inserted a hollow plastic tube through the vocal cords in the trachea.

Quickly, she removed the scope and inflated the balloon at the tip of the endotracheal tube which kept it in place. With great haste, she turned up the oxygen and gave the bag five rapid bursts of compression, pushing oxygen into Connie's lungs. The insertion process had temporarily interrupted all air exchange. Although it took Bella less than a minute to accomplish this, intensity and concentration played tricks with time. She then placed a stethoscope over Connie's chest and was satisfied that the tube was properly placed. She heard the unobstructed "swish" of gas moving through the tube and lungs. Bella smiled, the scar returned to her chin and she relaxed.

There were three nurses in the room. Two of them were already scrubbed and gowned. Everyone wore green caps hiding the hair and white cloth masks to cover the face. The scrub nurses were arranging instruments. One would hand these instruments as needed by Dr. Beatty. The other would act as first assistant, holding retractors as he worked.

The third nurse was the circulator, getting freshly sterilized instruments and materials for the operation. She also helped everyone else get into their sterile gowns and gloves.

Marjorie, the circulating nurse, was a tall, thin girl of about twenty-two. The loose-fitting green cotton dress that was the uniform of the operating room hung straight down from her broad shoulders. It reached to just above her knees. The same size dress reached almost to Bella's ankles.

Marjorie pulled the sheet and exposed Connie's body. Connie's full breasts sagged out to the sides. There were no stretch marks on her firm, flat abdomen. Her chest moved up and down gently with each respiration controlled by Bella.

In the recumbent position, the blue vein in her left leg was completely invisible.

"Which leg is it?" Marjorie asked as she studied Connie's legs.

"I don't know," Barbara said. She was the instrument nurse. Her face, head and body were hidden by gown, cap and mask. Only her eyes, carefully made up with green eyeshadow, were distinctive.

"Here, look in the chart," Bella said.

"It's the left," Marjorie said while still reading from the hospital record. She handed the record back to Bella.

"Should I prep the leg now?" Marjorie asked.

"No, better wait for Dr. Beatty," Barbara commented as she placed a tray containing various sized hemostats arranged in neat rows upon the Mayo stand.

A minute later, Dr. Beatty pushed in the door with his back. His dripping hands were held at chest level in front of him. Aggie, the other scrub nurse, handed him a sterile towel to dry his hands.

Dr. Beatty ceremoniously dried his hands

and then threw the towel to Marjorie. Aggie opened a green gown and held it up for him to step into. While she put his gloves on, Marjorie tied the back of the gown.

"Why isn't this leg prepped?" Beatty was annoyed as if it were the first time he had looked at the patient lying there.

"We were waiting for you," Barbara said flatly.

"Well, go ahead and do it!" he shot back at her.

"There's no need to shout," Barbara returned as she snapped a sterile towel between her hands.

"Marj, please hold up her leg," Barbara said. "It is the left leg, isn't it?" she turned to Beatty who was waiting impatiently.

"Right," Beatty answered and the three nurses froze. "Correct, I mean."

The three nurses giggled nervously. Marjorie lifted Connie's left leg above the table by holding onto the toes with one hand. Barbara handed a cup full of povidine and a gauze sponge folded in a long metal holder to Dr. Beatty.

He accepted it shaking his head. "I'll have to change my gown and gloves after this," he said.

He began painting the leg with the antiseptic povidine. Starting above the groin, he worked his way down the thigh, letting the dark brown liquid drip around the leg onto the table. When the sponge dried out, he stuck it back into the small cup.

"Stop!" Barbara pointed a finger at him. "That's contaminated now. I'll give you another sponge stick and some fresh povidine."

"What are you making such a fuss about?" Beatty questioned.

Barbara walked over and took the used sponge stick from him. She gave him a fresh one and took away the contaminated antiseptic.

There are aspects of prepping a patient for surgery that seem to be derived from some ancient religious ritual. Povidine is an antiseptic and will kill most of the bacteria most of the time but not all of the bacteria all of the time. Ritual requires going from sterile to contaminated and forbids going from contaminated to sterile. The dried sponge had touched unsterile skin and returned to the cup of povidine. This made the povidine unclean.

Beatty continued with a fresh sponge stick and a new cup of povidine. He worked on the back side of the thigh without having to bend over very much; he was only five foot four. In street clothes, he looked taller because of the thick soles and the two-inch heels of his "elevator shoes." In twenty years, those shoes would be very stylish; at that time they served only his own vanity.

He was starting to bald with advance

rapidity. The process had started in his twenties. By thirty, he was combing his hair to carefully cover ever-widening areas of baldness. Now in his early forties, he struggled vaingloriously to keep the thinning strands of hair in place.

"This leg is getting heavy," Marjorie complained. Beatty ignored her. He painted the leg down to the foot. As he finished, it looked like he purposely painted her hand with the last swab.

Marjorie couldn't move yet. She still had to hold up the leg until sterile sheets were placed on the table under the leg.

Barbara handed Dr. Beatty one end of a folded sheet, which they opened and carefully placed on the table under the left leg and over the right one. As Marjorie lowered the leg, Aggie caught the foot in a double layer of towels which she wrapped around the top and secured with a sharply pointed towel clamp. The draping was completed by covering the torso with sheets. Only the brown-stained groin and lower left limb were left exposed.

Beatty approached the table and placed a gloved hand on the left leg. His gown was stained with povidine.

"You wanted to change your gown and gloves," Barbara reminded him.

"Forget about it," he waved his hand at her. "Let's get started already and stop wasting so much time with all this nonsense!"

There was nothing for her to do. She could take only so much flak from a man like Beatty and then she gave up. It wasn't her job to supervise the surgeon, she was there to help him. She slapped the handle of the scalpel into his palm.

The first cut went deep into the thigh. Instead of using the belly of the blade, Beatty had angled the scalpel too sharply and the point of the blade sliced down deeper than he could see. Blood rapidly rose up the sides of the wound, mixing with the brown stain of povidine. The red was dominant as it streaked along the leg.

"Clamps! Hurry up! Give me some clamps!" Beatty called anxiously. One, two, three clamps were thrust into the wound blindly adhering to fat, flesh and skin without staunching the flow of blood. There was no more room in the small wound for another clamp. He removed the three useless ones and stuck his finger in the hole. It was more effective for the time being.

He picked up the scalpel he had dropped on the sheets. The incision was extended another two inches. It was already twice the size of the "little nick" he had promised Connie. More blood flowed along the cut edges but this was slow and would eventually stop.

He forced a large hemostat beneath the finger which was compressing the source of major bleeding. He opened the jaws of the hemostat widely but unseen under his hand. Then he closed them. He lifted his finger from the wound very slowly. The bleeding stopped. Using the scalpel, he cut down around the clamp to expose the area more widely.

"Goddam!" he said proudly. "Lookit here, right on the saphenous vein."

The nurses ignored him and looked at each other instead.

"Kelly," he said holding out a hand. Barbara handed him the requested clamp and he applied it below the first one. Then he cut the vessel between the two clamps.

"Stripper," he said. "This is going real good." He waited while Barbara carefully picked out a long wire with a bulb on one end.

"Caught you napping. I bet you've never seen anyone get down to the vein this fast," he boasted.

Barbara handed him the vein stripper. There was nothing for Aggie to do. Indeed, she had never seen anyone approach a vein stripping this way. The dissection was usually much slower and much more careful. There were five tributaries draining into the saphenous vein. Each one was usually isolated and tied off before the saphenous vein was tied and stripped.

Beatty passed the metal wire down the vessel. From the length of wire that disappeared into the lumen, it seemed to stop somewhere just below the knee. He tugged hard. Initially, there was some resistance and then it suddenly gave way. The wire returned with a blood vessel telescoped over it. He handed the wire and the vessel to Barbara.

"That's all there is to that!" he tried hard to gain admiration from the nurses who were purposely silent. He saw himself quite differently than his audience did.

"We're closing, Bella dear," he called over the sheets separating Dr. Czerny from the surgical field.

"Don't 'Bella dear' me," she retorted standing on tiptoe to get a view of what was happening. He started closing the wound. Bella started working quickly, too. She increased the oxygen flow, closed the halothane valve and began squeezing the black bag rapidly and as hard as she could.

Beatty finished before Connie was awake.

"Let's wrap the leg in Ace bandages," he ordered mildly.

The circulating nurse was ready with the light brown elastic bandages. Starting at the foot, the bandage was unrolled and snugly wrapped over the skin. The first roll unwound to just below the knee. The second bandage unrolled up to her groin. The entire lower limb was hidden beneath the light brown elastic bandage.

Beatty was too pleased with himself. He smiled at everyone as he went about the hospital. His pleasantries caught the hospital personnel off-guard. To his face, they all exchanged greetings in kind but after he left almost everyone commented. "What's with him today?"

At his office, three hours later, the sky caved in. He had no way of knowing the telephone ring would be followed by a thunderbolt. It was Jim Watson, the hospital's staff pathologist, on the line.

"I've got some bad news for you," Dr. Watson said in soft expectant tones. It was a funereal voice appropriate with irreversible bad news.

Watson had no sympathy for Beatty. He had him caged without Beatty knowing it. When he told him the news, the clanging door burned the ears and soul of Dr. Emery Beatty.

"That vein you stripped out this morning was an artery," Watson continued in the same calm way. He stopped. It was Beatty's turn now.

"You're crazy! It can't be," Beatty protested rancorously.

"It is and your patient has a very serious problem right now," Watson said.

"You're out of your fucking mind!" Beatty shouted. The terrible consequences began to sink in. "You haven't had time to make sections of that specimen yet!"

"I will but I don't have to," Dr. Watson said with a cutting edge to his voice. "That's a big artery, probably the femoral artery."

Beatty's mouth was dry as if someone had given him a cupful of sand to drink. His skin crawled and it felt cold and wet.

"You can't be sure," he mumbled. Watson couldn't hear him but before he could ask, "What?" Beatty hung up the phone.

Beatty rushed out of his office to the hospital as fast as he could. The hospital was congested with visitors. Each bedside was surrounded by two or three friends and family. Beatty pushed through the crowded elevator to get off at the second floor. The nurse in charge of the floor saw him hurrying down the corridor toward Connie Belanger's room. She called after him and sounded anxious enough for him to stop.

"I've had to medicate Mrs. Belanger twice," she referred to pain medication. "Could you increase the dose?"

"I'm going to see her now," he walked on. The nurse followed him. "You don't have to come," he advised her abruptly.

Tom Belanger was sitting beside his wife's bed holding her hand. She looked quite pale and was in a drugged stuporous state. She moaned and occasionally turned her head from side to side.

Belanger stood up when Beatty came into

the room. Beatty just looked at him without speaking. His attitude worried Belanger.

"She seems to be in a lot of pain," Belanger reported, hoping something could be done.

"The nurse told me," Beatty said. "Let me take a look at her."

Beatty pulled the curtain around the bed to exclude Tom Belanger from his examination. Belanger cooperated fully by getting out of his way for Connie's sake.

Beatty pulled back the sheets. He couldn't tell a thing with the leg completely covered with Ace bandages. He unwrapped the foot part. That was all he needed to see.

The foot was gray and icy to the touch. It wasn't like death—it was dead! The lower limb from just below his incision to the toes was a piece of meat and bone. By tomorrow, the gray would become black as the skin rotted with dry gangrene.

Beatty was shaken and his hands sweated profusely. He wiped them on his jacket and then re-bandaged the foot. Connie had groaned only once during the manipulation of her leg. She twisted her body and bent the other leg. The left one was immobile.

Tom Belanger waited for him as he emerged from behind the curtain. He looked up at Tom who was just under six feet tall. The husband's brown eyes narrowed perceptively as his anxiety grew. Beatty cleared his throat and looked grim.

"There's a serious complication," Beatty said. His voice became firmer as he straightened his shoulders and buttoned his suit coat. "I wish Connie had listened to me and come in sooner. I begged her for two years but she kept putting it off. I was afraid this might happen."

Tom's foot began to tap uncontrollably against the floor. He had to sit down as his knees weakened. Beatty could now look down at him.

"A serious blood clot has developed in her leg. This was the danger all along. It could have killed her but she came in just in time. Tom, I'll tell you the truth. I don't want to hide anything."

"Wait a minute," Tom looked up horrified. "Should she be hearing this?"

"She's quite out of it right now," Beatty assured him. "Tom, I'm going to do everything I can to save her but she might lose the leg. I'm going to need help on this. I'd like your permission to call in a vascular surgeon from New York. He can be here in two hours."

"Oh my God!" Tom said covering his eyes. "Do whatever you have to. Even if she has to be transferred to New York."

"I'll do my best," he placed his hand gently on Tom's shoulder.

On the way out, Beatty stopped at the nurse's desk.

"Miss Gallatin," he called to get the

nurse's attention. She was talking to a wrinkled old lady dressed in a hospital issue gown. The patient had wandered out of her room and couldn't find her way back.

"Just a minute," the nurse said. "Gail, will you take Mrs. Wershub back to her room?"

Beatty's irritation grew. The other nurse came to escort Mrs. Wershub so Miss Gallatin could attend to Beatty.

"Miss Gallatin, could you please answer me when I ask for something?" Beatty drummed his fingers on the counter top.

"Sure," the pretty young girl with blond hair answered. "Go ahead and ask."

"Give Mrs. Belanger another hundred of Demerol," he said.

"She just got fifty an hour ago," Gallatin indicated she thought another hundred was too much too soon.

"Didn't you say she was in pain?" His eyes fired with anger by her seeming insubordination.

"Maybe another twenty-five," Gallatin suggested. "What's wrong? Patients don't usually have this much pain with a vein stripping."

"Thrombophlebitis," Beattie said. "Give her another seventy-five and stop playing doctor. Where's the order book. I'll write it!"

She handed him the doctor's order book. He wrote the order for the medication to be given immediately.

He almost ran to the surgeons' lounge adjacent to the operating room. It was on the same floor but in another wing on the opposite side of the hospital.

At three-thirty in the afternoon, the surgeons' lounge was deserted. So was the operating room. Dr. Beatty searched through his wallet for the business card he wanted. *The Medical Protection Company, Charles Zukoff, Agent*. That was his malpractice insurance company and he called immediately.

After Zukoff managed to calm him down, Beatty carefully told him what happened in detail.

"Tough case," Zukoff sighed through the phone. "You must have a vascular surgeon look at it and try to save the leg."

"I told you the leg was dead, gone! Don't you understand?" Beatty became angry again.

"It'll be worse if you take the leg off without a consultation," Zukoff quietly advised him.

"It'll have to come off just the same," Beatty commented with woeful resignation.

"It'll look better when we have to settle," Zukoff insisted. "Ask your lawyer if you don't believe me."

"Who's my lawyer?" Beatty said. "I thought your company supplies the lawyer."

"We do, but in this case I strongly suggest that you get your own lawyer too," he said. "You're only covered for a hundred thousand."

"I thought it was three hundred thousand," Beatty said indignantly.

"It's a hundred thousand maximum for each occurrence, three hundred thousand total for any premium period," Zukoff sounded like he was reading from the policy. "It'll cost you a lot more than that."

"How much more?" Beatty asked. He wiped his head nervously, destroying the neat arrangement of the thinning hair across his scalp. The growing bald spot was quite evident.

"They could ask for a million but will probably settle for half," he said. "Will she live?"

"Of course she will! It wasn't that bad," Beatty said.

"In that case, they'll also ask for lifetime payments, rehabilitation and compensatory payments for the children. You say she's only in her thirties. Well, if she was a little old lady in her eighties, it would be much less. Might even be covered by the policy if she had some other illness to take her away. Let me know the name of your lawyer when you get one."

"Damn!" Beatty said after he slammed down the phone. He thought he was covered. Everything he had would be gone. He paced back and forth, then into the silent operating room, cursing the day he had ever walked in there.

The cold windowless walls along the central corridor of the operating suite were like those of a tomb. In the dim light, the pastel blue reflected only slate gray interrupted by black shadows. His wooden heels clicked against the floor tiles and returned a muffled echo. He walked past the deep scrub sink with its row of gleaming faucets standing out above the well. He fought a strong urge to vomit over the white porcelain.

He started to sweat in the cold, air-conditioned operating suite. Then felt terribly cold. Every door was closed. He turned about to stare quickly at each one, feeling they were bolted and he was trapped.

There was no surgeon in the world who could restore the dead flesh hanging from Connie Belanger's hip. There was no faith healer or satanic magician who could reverse the entropy of death in that limb. Restoring the blood flow with a dacron graft would not help. Flooding the limb with the blood of Carthage, Gettysburg, Ypres, Normandy, My-Lai and even Armageddon would not restore it to life.

Anesthesia. The word was printed in block letters, big white letters cut into a blue background and hung on the door. She could have died from anesthesia. If she never woke up, the limb would be just like the rest of her, he thought. If she died, the greater catastrophe would obscure his mistake. It happens to people in surgery. Obscure causes of death. Unexpected causes, unpreventable causes for which no one is blamed.

He pushed open the door to the anesthesia room. The light switch was just inside the door. The overhead fluorescent lamps flickered to life and were reflected from the glass cabinets lining the four walls. A row of six carts containing the anesthesia equipment stood to one side of the room.

Beatty walked over to one of the small two-tiered carts. Each was made of stainless steel tubes that supported a rectangular tray about a foot and a half long. Endotracheal tubes, laryngoscopes and syringes were neatly arrayed on a clean cloth towel. Behind the tray, suspended from the steel tubing were small rectangular baskets containing solutions of medications.

They were small bottles with rubber caps marked with a double circle of molded rubber forming a bullseye. The rubber in the center of the bullseye was thinner so it could be more easily penetrated by a hypodermic needle to draw out the clear watery solution. The solutions looked exactly alike, all appearing to be nothing more than crystal-clear water, but each one was different. Each contained minute amounts of powerful drugs dissolved in water or weak salt solution. Each vial was identified by a printed label: atropine, scopalamine, pentathal, saline, succinyl choline.

Dr. Beatty took the full bottle of succinyl choline and a syringe from the cart. He left quickly. Tomorrow morning, Bella Czerny would check her cart carefully to be sure she was well-prepared to give anesthesia. She would shake her head, cluck her tongue and mumble to herself about the inefficiency of the nurse who was responsible for stocking all the carts with drugs. Then she would go to the cabinet and get a fresh bottle of succinyl choline without telling anyone.

Dr. Czerny couldn't begin anesthesia without succinyl choline. It is a synthetic analogue of curare. It blocks the transmission of the impulse between the nerve ending and the muscles.

A thick heavy nerve runs through the arm and down the leg like a coaxial cable giving off strands of fibers which branch repeatedly. Each branch gets smaller and smaller until they are indistinguishable from the muscle fibers. To the naked eye, they seem welded or spliced together like an electrical cord to some machine.

In the microscopic milieu, nerve and muscle never join. They remain separated by space, a lake of chemical solution, a placid cauldron of chemical reactions.

The nerve impulse arrives at this shore at full gallop and crashes into the lake. Progress is slowed by the swim across to the distant shore where the gallop begins again once dry footing is regained. Succinyl choline and curare are like quicksand, preventing the impulse from crossing over from nerve to muscle.

The brain remains alert. It can keep sending signals to the muscles but they never get the message. Arms and legs don't respond. The muscles of the chest wall and the diaphragm are effectively paralyzed. The voluntary control of air exchange between the lungs and the atmosphere stops.

Succinyl choline is not an anesthetic. Sensory pathways back to the brain are quite different. Under anesthesia induced by other drugs, air exchange is maintained by mechanically forcing air in and out of the lungs through the endotracheal tube while the muscles are paralyzed.

Succinyl choline is a complete muscle relaxant, so effective that the muscles lose their tone so the surgical wound stays open with easy retraction. By keeping the door open, it makes any abdominal surgical procedure easier and faster.

Without an endotracheal tube and a

mechanical breathing device, succinyl choline is a deadly poison. It acts faster than curare. The victim remains alert until she has suffocated. Suffocation occurs in the midst of precious air which can't be moved into the lungs. It's like drowning without water, or being smothered by an ephemeral film.

Beatty got back to Connie Belanger's room without being seen. The nurses were still giving report to the oncoming shift. They were all gathered in a small conference room. One nurse's aide was available and she was in another patient's room. Tom Belanger had just 'left to see his kids home from school.

Connie was awake when Beatty walked into her room. When nurse Gallatin came in earlier to give the additional Demerol ordered by Beatty, she found Connie asleep so she withheld the medication. Now the Demerol was wearing off.

Connie's eyes were heavy with the aftereffects of the Demerol but she opened them as Dr. Beatty stood at her bedside. Her skin was pale, her lips puffy and dry.

"Oh," she moaned and tried to move but was achored by the dead leg. She writhed as her face twisted in pain. "Doctor," her voice cracked, "it hurts so much."

"I have something for you, Connie," he

held up the vial of succinyl choline with the syringe underneath stuck into it up to the hub of the needle. "This will make it all go away."

With little effort, her eyes closed as she seemed to sigh with gratitude. Beatty injected ten cc's of the solution through the IV tubing that went into a vein. Carefully, he recovered the needle with its sheath and placed the vial and syringe in his pocket.

Fifteen seconds later, Connie's eyes snapped open. Pain had turned to fear. Her lower jaw moved down as if in slow motion. It closed even slower. Her lip made a feeble twisting motion and then stopped.

She continued to stare at Beatty who stood by, studying her chest for signs of respiration. She was totally immobile. Her eyes were fixed at dead center even when he moved away. Only the automatic, involuntary pupillary muscles constricted from fear.

The pillow kept her head propped up as she continued to stare straight ahead. Beatty moved away from her eyes. He stood behind her and placed his hands an inch away from her mouth and nose. Air flow was undetectable.

He pulled his hand away and balled it into a tight fist. His pupils were constricting as he became impatient. Someone might walk in but he had to be sure now. How long could it take for her to die? About as long as she could stay under water.

He looked at his watch. A couple of minutes more. Her lips were darkening with a blue hue. Five minutes had passed. Her eyes were still open and the pupils were dilating. Another minute and the pupils were as wide as a doll's. He reached over to close the lids. Her head flopped off the pillow. He left the room unseen.

TEN

Afternoon office hours dragged for Dr. Josephson. Every patient had to talk to him about some pressing problem. He was having difficulty listening. His concentration wandered from tales of epic bowel movements, aches and pains of little consequence except for the need for more regular exercise, mortal struggles between diets and calories.

He was late because he had stayed behind at the hospital, hoping to run into Mike Bradley or Emery Beatty. It was wasted time, as he had seen neither of them. He had to learn more from Charlie before he could broach the subject directly with Dr. Bradley. In any case, he had no idea what he would say to Dr. Beatty. In the meantime, his patients noticed a change in the usually sympathetic Dr. Josephson.

"Thank you very much," Mrs. Olga Hirsch said as she folded the prescription just handed to her by Dr. Josephson.

She was a pleasant-looking woman in her late sixties. Short and slightly overweight, she still had a pretty round face that suggested she once was considered "cute." Burt was sure her golden hair, swept up from behind and piled in broad curls atop her head, was colored with dye.

"What should I do about my husband?" she settled back in the chair in front of Burt's desk. "Forty-two years we're married and just now I'm finding out what kind of man he is. When he was working, I hardly ever saw him. Now he's retired I first find out what kind of bastard he really is."

The phone rang and Burt hoped it was Charlie. Each time the phone rang that afternoon, he listened as Karen answered it. He was afraid Karen would tell Charlie to call back because he was with a patient.

Mrs. Hirsch thought he was thinking

about her problem. He was thinking about Charlie instead. She waited for him to comment. She expected at least some change in his facial expression, but he had other things on his mind.

"What should I do with him?" she finally went on. "He won't go anywhere. He sits home like a lump of coal. Doctor? Doctor, did you hear what I said?"

"Take a lover," Burt said.

"What?" Mrs. Hirsch said as if she hadn't heard him correctly. "I should take a lover? Who could I get?" She wasn't opposed to the idea. It just didn't sound practical.

"I didn't mean it literally," he said. He regretted his off-the-cuff remark. "Find your own interests but find something he would like, too. And then go and do it. He'll follow soon enough."

Burt got up and walked around his desk to her. She stood next to him. With a little poke in his belly she said, "You're getting skinny, Dr. Josephson."

Josephson blushed. He stepped out of his office quickly. Mrs. Hirsch followed him to Karen's desk.

"I'll see Mrs. Hirsch again in a month," he told Karen and walked back past the patient in the narrow hallway.

"Good-bye, Doctor," Mrs. Hirsch smiled and waved at him.

A few minutes later he went back to

Karen's desk.

"What was Mrs. Hirsch so happy about?" the diminutive Karen asked, looking up at Burt.

"How should I know?" Burt said quickly then added. "I make everyone happy. How many more lucky patients do we have today?"

Karen swiveled her stool around to the desk and ran her finger down the appointment book.

"Four more until supper break and then eight after that," she replied, turning back to him.

"We have hours tonight?" Burt groaned. "Call everyone and cancel them. I've got to be home tonight. Who's scheduled?" he asked as he leaned over, almost crushing Karen against the desk. After checking the list he said, "They can all come tomorrow."

"We're closed tomorrow night," Karen protested sharply.

"So now we're open tomorrow night," he said just as hard as she did. "Just call them!"

"I won't be here tomorrow night," she said.

Burt thought about it for a moment. That was okay with him. He'd beg Loretta to help him out. It was her fault he wanted to be home tonight, anyway. Maybe she would like working in the office if she tried it.

"I'll work alone," he said, keeping his plan to himself.

"You're on call tonight and you're also covering for Dr. Simon," she reminded him. "Should I call him too?"

"Yeah, get him for me but don't say anything. I'll speak to him myself." He picked up the next patient's chart. "Send Mr. Clementi into room three and then start calling."

Burt continued working in his distracted state. With Karen on the phone rearranging appointments, the telephone couldn't ring. He worried about that. If Charlie was trying to get him, the phone would be busy and he might give up today.

He had been reluctant when Charlie first presented the problem to him. There seemed to be nothing to it except Charlie's suspicions. He had learned nothing definite to change his first impression, but now there were rough edges sticking out of the neat defense he had constructed against Charlie's views.

He was also irritated by what he perceived to be a dramatic change in Loretta. She seemed too intense, too distant and separate from him because of this job. Of course, she had always been energetic and determined, but this was different as far as he was concerned. Before it had always been for him or the children, the house or the practice. It occurred to him that she was doing this strictly for herself. But why?

Karen interrupted to tell him Dr. Simon was on the line.

"Nate, take my calls for me tonight, huh?" he asked gently.

"Jeez, I can't Burt," Nate begged off. "I was up last night with a kid in diabetic coma. A twenty-two-year-old girl never diagnosed before. Her mother found her, thought she had taken an overdose. I really can't do it tonight."

"For me, Nate, please," he begged softly. "Remember, you saved my life once when you pulled me out of the surf at Far Rockaway."

"What has that got to do with it?" Nate sounded off indignantly. "I'm not Chinese or a redskin. You still owe me for that one."

"Okay, this weekend we'll go to the beach and I'll pull you out of the surf but cover for me tonight," Burt pleaded. "At least until midnight."

"Are you okay?" Nate sounded worried. "Is your gallbladder kicking up again? Tell the truth, Burt. If you're not feeling well, I'll cover for you."

"I'm not sick! There's nothing wrong with my gallbladder," Burt said angrily. "I'll sign out to you from six to midnight, that's all I'm asking."

"What about your office hours?" Nate stalled.

"I cancelled them."

"Burt, level with me. Are you stepping out on Loretta?" Nate probed quietly as if someone could overhear them.

"Are you crazy?" Burt shouted into the telephone. "Whatever gave you that idea?"

"I don't know," Nate said innocently. "Two weeks ago you ran off to New York in the middle of the day. Now you want me to cover for you when you're supposed to be in your office. Yesterday, I saw you having a long talk with Chimento. I don't care what you do with your life but you're doing it stupidly."

"I happen to know Chimento was working that day I went to New York," Burt said confidently. "I remember because she liked my suit a lot."

"I have nothing against her," Nate apologized. "But it's stupid to get involved like that at the hospital. Everyone starts talking about it."

"So far, you're the only bigmouth I know," Burt said. "Look this has nothing to do with Chimento or anybody else. I'll be home with Loretta tonight, okay? It's very important for us to talk together. She's planning on taking a job in the ICU working nights. Do you get the picture?"

"I think that's great," Nate said. "You're a chauvinistic pig if you try to stop her."

"Just get out of my life and mind our

own business," Burt said, genuinely annoyed. "I'm signing out to you."

"Okay, but only until midnight. If you can't make her by then after all these years, just forget it."

"Fuck you," Burt said softly as he hung up.

Burt felt some satisfaction. At least he could rely on Nate Simon, but he still had to find out more from Charlie. One way or another, he would eventually tell Nathan everything. The way he told him depended on how much solid evidence Charlie could come up with.

Where the hell was Charlie? Burt wanted to tell Loretta about it tonight. He knew he was too preoccupied with this Beatty business to discuss anything else with her sensibly. Loretta always rallied around him whenever he faced a tough problem. She wouldn't let him down now if this problem was as serious as Charlie thought.

At last, Charlie called.

"Ed Martin was very impressed with you," Charlie said as if Burt were applying for a job.

"Why should he be impressed?" Burt said, fencing with Charlie.

"He just was," Charlie said. "He said you sounded like a careful man. That's very important."

"Could we cut the crap, Charlie?" Burt said plainly. "I have a lot other things on my mind so let's get right down to how you got onto Beatty's tail and why."

"Okay, I'll tell you all I know," Charlie began slowly. "I never lied to you so whatever I've told you before is exactly how I got interested in Beatty."

"But you didn't tell me everything," Burt prodded him.

"I didn't tell you everything," Charlie admitted contritely. "First, I had to see how you would react."

"What did you expect?"

"Several things," Charlie said calmly. "You could have swallowed the whole story just as I gave it to you. In that case, you would have attacked Beatty publicly. It would have brought everything into the open and nothing would be accomplished. Beatty would deny the whole thing. Perhaps the family would sue. Then the whole thing would get buried in the courts for years and years.

"You could have gone directly to Beatty. Don't get me wrong. I mean you could have if you were a different kind of person. Some other doctor might have gone to Beatty and warned him. I'm not sure what could be accomplished by that but it would make things much more difficult for me."

"You did just what I hoped for. You looked at the record. You asked some discreet questions and used good judgement. You're a careful man."

"How do you know who I talked to or what I did?" Burt asked suspiciously, wondering if he was under observation.

"By the way you questioned Martin and your reaction to his answers," Charlie answered enthusiastically. "You have the right instincts when you ask questions but you can't hide your reactions to the answers."

Burt wanted to protest. He wanted to tell Charlie how a physician asks a question determines the quality of the response.

"Get on with it, Charlie," he said instead. "You presented me with a conclusion that Beatty was a murderer. Now I want your reasons."

"Neither Ed Martin or Jack Wishard could get an interview with Beatty." Charlie went on. "It was no big deal. They wanted some first hand information about the Demaris family from the doctor. They wanted to know how the family reacted to the treatment and restrictions of tuberculosis. They simply wanted to know how much of it was truly essential and how much was left over from another era? How much did their family physician tell them?

"Beatty's nurse gave them the appointment and Ed Martin went down to see him. Beatty was cordial at first but became more irritated after Martin started asking questions. That was when he threw Martin out of the office.

"Beatty's attitude only aroused Martin's curiosity. He got a hold of Demaris' hospital records and wanted Beatty to explain the discrepancy. Beatty's nurse had strict orders not to allow any reporters and especially Martin into the office. Martin followed Beatty around for a day. He finally cornered him in the surgeons' dressing room at Townbrook Hospital.

"Beatty bolted out of there, leaving his locker door open. Martin searched the locker and found a vial of succinyl choline sitting on the shelf inside the locker. He didn't know what it was but he took it with him anyway. It seemed like a strange thing to be sitting there in the locker."

"What's so strange about a doctor having medication?" Burt interrupted.

"Do you know what succinyl choline is?" Charlie asked.

"Of course I do!" Burt said. "But Ed Martin didn't know. It could have been any kind of medicine as far as he was concerned."

"He was looking for an angle," Charlie said. "Beatty had already acted peculiar so he was looking for anything else about him that was peculiar. The label on the bottle said 'For Intravenous Use Only.' Maybe Beatty was a drug addict or dispensing drugs illegally. It doesn't matter. Martin wanted to know what it was and what Beatty was doing with it."

"Martin learned what succinyl choline is used for and how it works. After he spoke to Dr. Bradley, Martin suspected Beatty was using the succinyl choline—"

"What did Mike Bradley tell him?" Burt cut in. "Why didn't Bradley indicate on the hospital record that Beatty had operated on Demaris?"

"You should ask Bradley yourself. Ed Martin was satisfied with the explanation in so far as he didn't think Bradley had anything to do with Demaris' death," Charlie said.

"He operated on him," Burt said. It was a smart aleck remark which had no bearing on the case. Burt knew it as soon as he said it. Charlie ignored it.

"Bradley was very upset over Demaris' death," Charlie said defensively. "It now looks like he was protecting Beatty but he had no sinister reason to do so. There may be some question of ethics involved but I'll leave that for you to decide.

"Potentially, there was a big story here. Martin and Wishard came to me for help. We started digging out some of Beatty's old cases, especially from around the time his privileges were suspended at Brady Memorial.

"There wasn't much to go on. At least there was nothing we could see from the records. We considered the possibility that much of it was written in medical jargon and that we couldn't read between the lines.

"One case in particular convinced us of this. The reason Beatty got kicked out of the operating room definitely involved a patient named Connie Belanger. He stripped out an artery instead of a vein and the patient died. I don't know if I'm saying this right. Could something like that kill a person?"

"I assume you mean a varicose vein but he got the artery instead," Burt offered. "It's terrible and the patient would lose a leg but something else had to kill her."

"There was a malpractice suit but it was settled by the insurance company out of court," Charlie sighed. "A committee, I believe it was the Executive Committee of the Medical Staff, accepted Beatty's resignation from the Surgery Department. In effect, he voluntarily gave up his surgical privileges at Brady Memorial."

"What did this Carol Belanger die of?" Burt asked.

"Connie Belanger," Charlie corrected him. "The death certificate listed pulmonary embolus as the immediate cause of death. The certificate was made out and signed Emery Beatty, M.D."

"I'll have them pull Belanger's chart for me tomorrow," Burt said, making a note of it on a memo pad he usually carried in his pocket.

"I can bring over a copy of her chart

right now," Charlie offered eagerly.

"No, I can't hang around right now. Something very important," Burt said forcefully. "The original is still at the hospital, isn't it?"

"Okay," Charlie conceded. Burt's tone left him no alternative. "Will you call me tomorrow afternoon?"

"You bet," Burt said.

ELEVEN

A delicious aroma hit Burt the moment he opened the back door leading into the kitchen. It made his mouth water and his stomach grumble with anticipation. The house was quiet. He peeked into the dining room.

The table was set for two, with a white table cloth and a single, perfect rose in a crystal vase in the center. He inspected the table more closely picking up a fork and replacing it. It was their good silver, and the wine glasses were Galway crystal.

"Loretta!" Burt called out. He walked down the hallway towards the bedrooms. Loretta came out to meet him.

"Stop bellowing," she smiled and put her arms around his neck.

She wore plum-colored pants with a diaphanous white blouse open to the middle of her chest. The decolletage was obscured by a bright golden pendant Burt had given her years ago. There was also something new which Burt found very attractive, even exciting.

She had cut her hair very short and had it curled tightly. Her smooth white neck stood out gracefully. Burt stared at the lovely neck as if he had never seen it before.

"Like it?" Loretta danced away as she patted the back of her hair. Burt continued to stare as if entranced. It was lovely, desirable and very interesting but he wasn't sure he liked it. His hesitation dampened Loretta's spirits only a bit.

"You better," she stopped dancing and pointed a long red fingernail at him, "I can't put it back," she said touching her hair again.

"I love it," Burt grinned, animated at last. He held his arms open and Loretta slipped in for a hug. "But what are we celebrating?"

"Nothing! Not a thing," she said looking up at him. In her flat-heeled slippers she barely came up to his chin. "I'll amend that, we're celebrating me and you. Slip into something more comfortable and I'll fix you a drink," she said in a fairly good imitation of Mae West.

Burt liked what he saw and the entire operation seemed smoothly planned. He knew he was being sandbagged, set up, outflanked, but whatever it was called, he liked it.

He decided to shower. After that, he ran a hand over his thick black beard. A shave wouldn't hurt.

"I never had a chance," he said to his face in the mirror. He whistled while he smoothed out his chin so the razor could run over it without nicking his skin.

"I hate taking advantage of her this way. She's so good," he said letting a smiling leer cross his lips. "Well, she'd be disappointed if I gave in too quickly. It could make her feel the effort was wasted. I should act tough," he said grimacing and making his neck muscles stand out.

"Serious," he said, letting his eyebrows sag. "No, that looks despondent. Despondent's not bad. Gets a lot of sympathy. But it's wrong," he sighed. "Don't get too heavy."

He wiped the remnants of the shave cream away with a towel, and slapped a few splashes of aftershave lotion on his cheeks. He put the cap back on the bottle and looked pleased with what he saw in the mirror. He unscrewed the cap and dowsed his ears and neck with a liberal amount of aftershave lotion.

A few minutes later he appeared wearing blue slacks and a pastel blue silky shirt. Loretta had a scotch on the rocks waiting for him. They sat down in the living room in front of the fireplace. Burt sat at one corner of the couch and Loretta at the other.

"To us," Burt lifted his glass and sipped. Loretta smiled.

"So, tell me," Burt said, "who were you expecting tonight?"

"Burt!" Loretta gasped almost choking on her wine. "What are you talking about?"

"You knew I was supposed to be working tonight," Burt said. "I was going to surprise you, sweep you off your feet and take you out to dinner. This is more beautiful than anything I had in mind. How did you know?"

"Nate Simon called about an hour ago," she said sheepishly, "I'm sorry if it ruined your plans."

"No, this is nicer than anything I planned," he said sincerely. "Nate Simon, Nate Simon, huh!"

"He only called to ask you about a patient," Loretta said. "I told him you were at the office and he said you were coming home. I was surprised but very happy you changed your schedule for me."

"Did he say that?" Burt asked.

"Yes, he did," Loretta said slightly worried. "You did, didn't you?"

"I did," Burt said warmly in a deep soft voice. He slid over to her side of the couch. "I wanted to talk to you, to say how—well, it doesn't seem to matter much right now."

"What doesn't?" she asked.

"Your job and working three to eleven. It's okay. We'll work it out," he said.

"I'm really sorry about that," she apologized. "It's hard for me, too, but that's the only job that was open in the ICU. It won't be for long, I promise," she pleaded sweetly. "Joan said I'm first in line to move up to the day shift because none of the other girls want to. And Marsha Halloran is getting married in two months. She's supposed to move to Michigan which means I'll get her job."

"Great! That's great," Burt smiled. "There's one more thing before I forget. Can you work for me tomorrow? I switched all my patients and Karen can't come in tomorrow night."

"Do I get paid?" Loretta raised an eyebrow.

"Paid? Why should you get paid? Of course, if you want to work full time, I'd pay you." Burt took another sip of scotch.

"I already have a job," Loretta straightened her shoulders proudly.

"I'll double your salary," Burt said quickly as he suddenly turned toward her and held her tightly around the waist. He put his face close to hers, almost touching her lips.

"Double?" she smiled letting her lips rub against his as she spoke. She kissed him hard and long. She held his neck gently and ran her other hand through his thick hair.

"What do you say?" he whispered in her ear and then nibbled her lobe. She squirmed beneath him. He pulled back and held her at arm's length. "Seriously, how about it?"

"I don't know," she said smiling broadly. "I've never been recruited this way before. What else does your company offer, Dr. Josephson?"

"Come on, Loretta!" Burt pulled away from her. He sat forward clasping his hands together, his elbows resting on his thighs. He sounded angry in subdued tones. "Why the hell do you need to work in that crummy hospital? What's the great attraction?"

"There's this really handsome doctor I'm crazy about," she said leaning on his arm reaching out to kiss his ear. "Hmm, he wears this great aftershave lotion."

She jumped up suddenly. "My roast is burning. Don't go away! I'll be right back."

Burt took a long sip of his scotch. He had

the feeling it wouldn't work before he tried but still he had to give it a shot. At least it was only for a few months. It would work out okay. When Loretta came back, he was still deep in thought.

"It's time for you to 'come on' Burt," she said. "You know I can't work for you on a regular basis. I mean I'll work tomorrow night but it's time for me to be myself again. You won't even notice, I bet, except that I'll be much happier and so will you. Now come on in to dinner and get rid of that long face."

"Okay," he surrendered with his hands up, "I knew I never had a chance . . ."

"You always have a chance with me," she sighed.

"I'm not brooding over your working," he said putting an arm around her shoulder as he escorted her into the dining room. "There's something quite different that has been on my mind for the last few days."

He held a chair away from the table as she sat down. A fruit cup was set at each place and the crown roast was steaming in the middle of the table.

"I've noticed you talking to yourself more than usual," Loretta said. "I thought it was because I was taking this job. Burt, please don't be upset about my going to work," she said intently as she reached over and placed her hand on his arm.

"I'm not. Got to work. We need the

money," he said facetiously. "Your son needs a new sports car."

"He does not! Which one? Did Arnold call you and ask for more money?"

"No, I'm just teasing you," Burt said. "He doesn't need anything right now. What are you going to do with the money anyway? It won't be as much as you think. You'll be in the fifty percent tax bracket, you know."

"Why do I have to pay so much?" Loretta asked indignantly.

"Because you're married to me. We file a joint return."

"That's not fair! It's my money and I should keep it."

"I want you to keep it too, honey, but at the end of the year they are going to ask for it back," he shook his head. "Don't worry about it. Just don't spend it all."

"Is that what's really bothering you?" she asked sympathetically.

"No, forget about what I said," he smiled. "There's something much more serious than that," he closed his eyes momentarily, then he looked up again at Loretta.

"It's that Charlie Dresden business again," she guessed, sounding pained. Burt looked surprised. "Isn't it?" Loretta asked.

"I suppose you can call it that," Burt said, "but it has gone beyond Charlie Dresden."

"I thought it would." She relaxed a little and began eating her fruit cup. "I could tell you were upset when you came home from New York. You were holding out on me."

"Not that afternoon," Burt excused himself. "I told you everything I knew. I didn't believe it but I told you what I thought about Charlie."

"And what made you change your mind?" Loretta was pleased with herself. "I told you Charlie was right."

Burt smiled, but hesitated to continue. He liked the little bundle of energy that made Loretta light up when she felt confident. It was just funny that she was gaining more confidence at his expense.

"I'm not certain he's right and neither are you," Burt said. "You're only reacting emotionally but I have changed my mind—"

"That's what I said," she interrupted, "you changed your mind."

"Let me finish, please," he said with more annoyance than pleading. "I think Charlie's suspicions are correct. There were some suspicious things, inconsistencies that only a suspicious mind would pay any attention to. That's how it stands now."

Burt stared at the wall across the table thinking about how he had arrived this far in his thinking. A few days ago, he thought Charlie was cynically interpreting every action as caused by the worst of motives. In other words, he had thought Charlie was full of shit. He still wasn't sure.

In any case, Loretta was the only one he felt he could confide in at this point. It had seemed natural to do so before, but now he was worried. Before, she had always seemed so pliable and responsive to him. Now, she wore her independence like a badge of honor. He wondered if he could trust her.

Burt burst into loud and uproarious laughter that made his shoulders shake and made tears come to his eyes. Loretta started laughing also without knowing why.

"Come on, stop!" she pleaded. "Tell me what's so funny?"

"We are. Everybody is funny," he said letting the laughter dissipate. "Do you love me?" he asked seriously.

"Yes, I do," she replied firmly and without hesitation.

"If I tell you something, will you swear not to tell anyone?" He gazed into her eyes. She stared back.

"Sure!" she said.

"Not even Nate Simon," he warned her. "I haven't said anything about this to him and I don't want him to know. Not yet, anyway."

"Oh, this has got to be good," she smiled. Two sunbursts flooded her eyes.

He had laughed at himself because he was contaminated by Charlie's thinking. He appreciated why Charlie was reluctant to give him all the information at once. It made sense to him now that he was faced with the same problem, but his own thinking interjected to make it more complicated. Just as Charlie felt about him, he didn't want Loretta to discuss this with anyone in case Beatty somehow got wind of it. There were still his own reservations. He didn't want the rumor mill to hurt Beatty if he was innocent.

"Charlie Dresden brought me a chart of a patient named Hugo Demaris," Burt began, Loretta took off her shoes, slipped her feet up under her and settled back to listen. "Demaris died in the ICU about three months ago. He was referred to Mike Bradley by Emery Beatty. Mike thought he had a stone in the ureter but it turned out to tuberculosis."

"TB?" Loretta asked, surprised. "Isn't that unusual?" she asked more softly.

"It is but that's beside the point," he said. "It's important because it's the way Charlie got involved but that's another story. Demaris developed a complication from surgery and then a coronary which put him in the ICU. It looked like a mild coronary but two days later he died."

"It happens," Loretta said sadly, but shrugged her shoulders.

"It happens," Burt sighed heavily, "In this case, it didn't just happen!" He caught himself getting too involved. "I mean, Charlie thought it didn't just happen. He thinks Emery Beatty killed Demaris."

"Burt!" Loretta exclaimed. "That's a horrible thing to say!"

"I didn't say it. Charlie said it," Burt defended himself. "I didn't think it was possible either until I looked at things a little differently. I asked a few discreet questions and found out that Beatty was the last one to see Demaris alive. Joan Chimento told me he was there just before the patient died but it wasn't in the record because officially he wasn't following the patient."

"What does Joan think?" Loretta was now very interested.

"I don't know," Burt said. "I didn't confide any of this to her. And you shouldn't, either. It's all very speculative at this point. There are a few other points I have to check out first. Charlie told me one of his associates found some succinyl choline in Beatty's locker at Townbrook Hospital. He still does surgery there and he probably operated on Demaris before Bradley did. So what do you think?"

"About what?" Loretta wondered what he expected of her.

"What do you think I should do next?" Burt said.

"Why should you do anything?" Loretta was puzzled by his involvement. "You must have left something out. I don't understand exactly what is going on here. If someone's been murdered, you should leave it to the police. And what does Charlie Dresden get out of all of this?''

"Don't be silly," Burt said. "I can't go to the police and tell them there are people dying in the hospital. How would that sound?''

"There's more than one?'' Loretta's eyes were aghast.

"There could be,'' Burt allowed. "Not recently, but this practice could go back several years.''

"Practice?'' Loretta unconsciously pulled on her newly short hair. "What kind of practice is that? How can you be so calm about this if you think it is possible?''

"Possible doesn't make it so,'' Burt said continuing his calm dissertation. "That's why I don't want you to talk to anyone about this until I can come up with some direct evidence. Understand?''

"I don't understand a word you're talking about,'' she said softly. "I don't care. Come to bed and make love to me. You get me so excited when you think so hard.''

"What about the roast beef?'' He teased, pleasantly surprised.

"I'll make you a cold sandwich later,'' she pinched his chubby cheek and pulled him out of the chair. He followed willingly.

"Don't forget the mustard," he grinned as she led him to the bedroom.

TWELVE

The next morning Dr. Josephson was in the hospital at a quarter to eight. He detoured from his usual first stop at the coffee room of the ICU to go to the operating room.

He felt like an uninvited visitor to some plush, exclusive club as he entered through the double glass doors of the operating suite. He passed the doors daily without giving the inner sanctum a second thought.

The lights were bright and the air cooler than in the hallway. Patients on stretchers were being wheeled into the operating rooms along each side of the central corridor. Nurses hurried in and out of rooms preparing for the first surgeries of the day. Everyone else was dressed in greens which made Burt feel even more conspicuous. He wasn't even sure he should be there in street clothes. But he wasn't completely awed by the gleaming blue tile and shiny metal corridors, it was like entering the ladies' shower room by mistake.

Harriet Goodhurst was happy to see him. She was the nurse-supervisor of the operating room. She got up from her desk when she saw him enter and came out to greet him. Harriet was a tall, good-looking woman close to sixty. She had been O.R. supervisor for over thirty years, which made her one of the few staff members still around who had attended the birth pangs of the new Brady Memorial Hospital.

"What can we do for you, Dr. Josephson?" she inquired cheerfully. Two young nurses skittered away down the corridor, giggling to each other. Harriet was rough and strict on the nurses in the O.R. when it came to work, but on a personal level, they could say anything they wanted to her and this greeting looked personal to them. Their snickers were not lost on Harriet.

"Am I in the right place with these clothes on?" Burt asked apologetically.

"You're fine," she said. "You only need greens to go through that door," she pointed straight ahead to where the patients were taken. "I suppose that's why we don't get any visitors from the medical department here. Are you here to watch one of your patients get sliced? I'll have one of the girls help you change your pants." She was only teasing him about the girls.

"No, I'm looking for Mike Bradley. Is he on the schedule this morning?" Burt returned her smile.

"He should be in the dressing room. Right through the door," she pointed the way for him. "Come back and see us more often. We like company."

Burt hear the toilet flush as he entered the surgeons' dressing room. A few seconds later Mike Bradley came out of the bathroom tieing the string on his pajama-like greens. He was tall, so he needed a large pair of pants but he was very thin so a medium would have been better for his waist. He bunched the green cotton cloth tightly around his waist with the drawstring.

"Hi, Burt," Bradley smiled, a little surprised to see him there.

Another voice was heard from behind a

row of lockers.

"Hey, Burt," it sounded large and booming. A moment later, Dr. Joe Pastorini appeared wearing boxer shorts that came almost to his knees. He was short, broad and muscular. His shorts were white and dotted with perfect red valentine hearts all over.

"Hey, what the hell is that?" Burt pointed to his shorts.

Pastorini pirouetted and curtsied holding on to the sides of his shorts. "You like 'em?" he asked threateningly.

"I love them, Joe. Where'd they come from? The Midnight Cowboy Thrift Shop?" Burt smiled.

"Watch it, Burt! My wife gave me these for my birthday. Don't get wise or I'll tell Loretta where she can buy them. Do you want to play tennis this Saturday? Nine o'clock."

"Sure," Burt said. "Nine o'clock.

Bradley was on his way out, "See you, Burt," he said, slapping him gently on the shoulder.

"Wait a minute," Burt turned quickly. "I have to talk to you."

Bradley closed the door and came back into the room. He was happy to talk to Burt, especially if it was about a patient he wanted to refer.

"Okay, see you Saturday," Pastorini said as he went back to change.

Two other surgeons came through the door and went to their lockers while Bradley waited to hear what Burt had to say. It wasn't the right place for Burt to open the subject. There were too many ears and mouths around. He nodded towards the door and walked out. Bradley followed him back to where Harriet Goodhurst had greeted Burt.

"This is no good either," Burt frowned, and seemed lost. Bradley frowned also but his face took on a more pained expression. He had a very volatile, elongated face with symmetrical creases runing from his eyes to his jaw. The lines could be extrapolated to his eyebrows to complete the circuit. Bradley took charge in the midst of Burt's confusion as to where to turn.

"In here," he took Burt by the elbow and lead him to a soundproof dictating room.

"This is nice," Burt said, inspecting the small room. There were three booths separated by waffled partitions. Each booth had a small desk, its own light and telephone for dictation.

Burt sat down and Bradley pulled another chair from an adjacent booth. He waited for Burt to start but Burt only made faces at him. He squeezed his lips together, raised his eyebrows, and sighed, but no words came out. Bradley was at a loss also since it was Burt who wanted to talk.

"Have you heard from Mr. Dixon lately?" Bradley asked, referring to a patient of Burt's who had been referred to him for surgery several months ago. It was a safe topic because Dixon had done very well after surgery.

"No, no I haven't," Burt said feeling very warm in the confined space despite the air conditioning. It was very difficult for him to come right out and say what was on his mind. What business did he have looking at Mike Bradley's records? Charlie's role in the matter seemed even less appropriate but Burt knew Charlie wouldn't be sweating if he were there interviewing Bradley.

He could mention Ed Martin. Bradley had already spoken to him. On the other hand, Martin could have been lying just to goad him into talking to Bradley about this case. Besides that, putting Martin into the picture might take away any advantage Burt had on a doctor-to-doctor relationship. Bradley would have his guard up so Burt decided that a little lie was the best way to make Bradley open up.

"I have a patient for you with chronic renal stones and a history of pulmonary tuberculosis," Burt began slowly.

"I'll be more than glad to see him," Bradley said, pleased to have a referral for possible surgery, "but why did we have to come in here for you to tell me that?"

"Because of the TB," Burt said. "It's inactive. He was treated for it twenty years ago but when anyone hears TB they get excited. I'd like him to be admitted here."

"It's no problem if his chest x-ray is normal," Bradley assured Burt. "I can admit him with a diagnosis of kidney stones."

"I was concerned about the relationship between his old TB and his kidney stones," Burt moistened his lips. "Is there any danger or special precaution to take because of the TB?"

Bradley pursed his lips and pulled his long chin. With his plastic facial muscles it looked like he was actually stretching his face.

"I'll have to see his pyelogram," Bradley said. "If there is any question of renal TB, we'll have to get urine cultures and wait eight weeks for the results. That's if he's in no distress."

"I haven't seen renal TB, have you?" Burt asked as he felt his heart beat faster.

"Yep," Bradley said despondently and let his huge eyes droop. "Three months ago, Emery Beatty sent me a case. What an asshole he is! He operates on this guy for acute appendicitis. Only the appendix is normal. Post-operatively, the patient is sicker than shit. A lot of flank pain so obvious that even Beatty knows to get an IVP. The pyelogram shows no function on the right and on a retrograde study there's complete obstruction of the ureter. Ninety-nine times out of a hundred, it's a stone you can't see. There is a history of TB in the family but when I asked the patient, he denied it. When I operated on the ureter, it was completely closed down with a abscess around it which later turned out to tuberculous. I'd swear that ureter had been clamped. I think Beatty not only missed the diagnosis but got into the ureter when he was searching for the appendix. There were silk sutures near the ureter."

"Did you mention this to anyone?" Burt probed, controlling his anxiety. The door was open and he decided to press for as much as he could get.

"You mean, report him? What am I, a detective?" Bradley raised his voice slightly. "Why didn't Jim Watson say anything? I sent him a biopsy containing silk sutures. There's no one to report to. Besides, you just get yourself tied up with a lawsuit. Who needs it?"

Bradley didn't mention that Beatty frequently referred patients to him. This also crossed Burt's mind but he decided not to mention it. Bradley's reasons were enough for him. What the hell was *he* doing acting like a detective, Burt wondered.

"If he had told me the patient had tuberculosis, I would have approached it differently. I would have done a planned, two-stage procedure. First, draining the abscess and diverting the urine, then coming back for a plastic repair of the ureter."

Bradley spoke enthusiastically and with the relief associated with confession. It was not only confession, but justification which shed the blame on someone else.

"I think Beatty is crazy," Bradley went on. "I spoke to the patient's wife and she said the two kids had TB. I told her myself that her husband had it. Beatty knew this but he told her her husband had cancer with little hope of surviving.

"He's crazy but he turned out to be right about survival. Two and a half weeks after surgery, the guys had a heart attack and two or three days later, died. I spoke to the wife and she says, 'Thank God he didn't have to suffer with cancer.'

"I tried to explain to her, to tell her it was TB, not cancer. I tried very hard to get an autopsy but she says, 'No, he's suffered enough.' "

Bradley was really agitated. He felt distress as he relived the agony of his patient and the family. Burt saw why Charlie had ruled out Bradley as being directly responsible for the death of Hugo Demaris. He sympathized with Bradley and considered telling him what Charlie thought of Demaris, but it wasn't time for that yet. Even though Bradley supported Charlie's theory, it didn't prove that Beatty had killed anyone. If Burt was going to be a detective, he was going to be a good one. Careful, that's what Charlie said. Burt was careful.

He told Bradley he would speak to his patient about surgery. If the patient agreed, he would send him to Bradley.

Burt walked down the hospital hallway staring at his feet, thinking about his options. He was being paged but ignored it. He recognized the number. "Dr. Josephson, call 220," the paging operator announced again. Someone wanted him in the ICU and he was on his way there.

As he turned a corner, he collided with a much shorter, bald-headed man who was hurrying in the opposite direction. The man practically bounced off Burt and looked up with an angry scowl. His eyes were wide-set and the pupils constricted with belligerency. He wore a dark blue three-piece suit with a gold chain cross his vest.

Burt was about to apologize for the collision but the man sidestepped him and kept on going around the corner before Burt could say anything. He had recognized Dr. Emery Beatty.

Burt stood there wondering if he should go after him. There were important matters to discuss. He had had Beatty on his mind as he was walking around the corner, but was so preoccupied that he didn't see him coming. Though he recognized Beatty immediately, it was almost like a deja vu and the coincidence caught him off guard. When Burt retraced his steps back around the corner, Beatty was gone. Probably down the staircase on the left.

Loretta and Joan were having an animated conference at the medicine cabinet when Burt walked into the ICU. Loretta was pointing at the far side of the unit. Burt looked and saw nothing unusual in that direction. Neither did Joan, who was concentrating on Loretta. Joan looked distressed by whatever Loretta was telling her. Loretta turned, saw Burt and stopped talking in mid-sentence.

"Burt, get over here!" she stage-whispered, waving frantically for him to hurry. Joan reacted in the same way. She moved her hands as if she were pulling him toward her. She even stamped her foot as he was slow to respond. They both came at him and met him half-way. Each one took an arm and hurried him along.

"Get in here," Joan said anxiously as they directed him toward the ICU conference room. Joan shut the door forcefully. Only the hydraulic transom prevented it from slamming.

"What's going on?" Burt demanded, amused and confused. They let his arms go. Joan had one hand on her hip and other pushing her hair back on the side of her head. Loretta was almost jumping up and down with agitation.

"Do you know who was just in here?" Loretta said as her face creased with lines of anxiety. "Emery Beatty!"

Burt looked sharply away from Loretta to Joan. It was obvious she had told Joan because Joan's face shared the same concern that Loretta's did.

"Why didn't you tell me about him?" Joan chastised him.

He turned away quickly to give Loretta a burning stare.

"I told you to keep this to yourself," he said in a soft biting voice.

"Don't yell at her!" Joan snapped. "What was she supposed to do?"

"She was supposed to mind her own business!" Burt turned in dismay and anger to Joan.

"Burt," Loretta said taking a short breath to calm herself, "that man snuck in here and went to Mrs. Lipton's bedside. He pulled the curtains around the bed so no one could see that he was doing!"

"What do you mean he 'snuck in here?'" Burt said. "He came in to see a patient. It is proper for him to pull the curtain if he's going to examine her!"

"He snuck in here, Burt!" Loretta insisted. "He didn't stop at the desk to check her chart. He walked straight for the cubicle and pulled the curtain. I just saw him as he was pulling it. Another second and I would have missed him."

"That doesn't mean he was sneaking," Burt shook his head. "Why did you say anything to Joan?"

"Because I'm in charge here!" Joan snapped at him.

"I had to call Joan," Loretta tried desperately to demonstrate the urgency for Burt. "I was alone at the medicine cabinet and I couldn't just leave the narcotic cabinet open. Besides, I didn't know what to do."

"This is what I was afraid of," Burt said calmly. He sat down on the straight-backed chair. "You're both getting hysterical over nothing."

Loretta and Joan looked at each other supportively. Burt had not meant to insult them but he felt the matter was too important to worry about personal feelings.

"Sit down! Both of you," he ordered. He pulled two chairs away from the table. With his long arms outstretched, his chest expanded and the concern burned on his face, he had the aura of a bull-ape demanding obedience. Besides that, the two women looked upon him as the instigator. They had no one else to turn to.

"What did you do to Dr. Beatty?" Burt looked sternly at Loretta.

"I didn't do anything to Dr. Beatty!" Loretta said. "I called Joan over and said I have to go into Mrs. Lipton with him."

"I had to know why," Joan jumped in.

"Loretta wasn't assigned to her. She was supposed to stay with the meds."

"After what you said last night, I couldn't leave him alone with her," Loretta said.

"What's wrong with Mrs. Lipton?" Burt asked.

"She has cancer. All over," Loretta said. "She had a choledochojejunostomy," the syllables stuck in her palate but she got them out slowly but correctly, "to relieve her jaundice."

"Who's the surgeon?" Burt continued his quiet inquiry.

"Dr. Pastorini," Loretta said. "She was referred to him by Dr. Beatty who did the original colon surgery a year ago."

"Could you get her chart for me?" he asked Joan. Joan responded quickly, relieved to be out of the spotlight.

"I spoke to you in the strictest confidence about Beatty," Burt whispered to his wife. She backed away from him but returned his glare.

"I'm sorry I had to tell Joan, but there was no other way," Loretta apologized.

"You overreacted," Burt said calming down a bit.

"But you said Beatty had to be stopped," Loretta said.

"When did I say that?" Burt said looking very surprised.

"In your sleep you said very distinctly,

"I have to stop Beatty!"

"Do I talk in my sleep?" Burt asked meekly.

"Yes, you do, Burt. You have for years," she said sympathetically, suggesting to him that he was a completely open book as far as she was concerned.

"What have I talked about besides Beatty?" he asked.

"A lot, Burt. A lot!" She bit her lower lip softly. Before he could find out what she meant, Joan came back.

"Here's the chart. Pastorini's op note just came back," Joan said. In one hand she held the chart. In the other, there was two typewritten sheets of paper. Burt took the chart and the operative report from her.

"What did you two do to Dr. Beatty?" Burt demanded. His tone had changed distinctly. He no longer sounded like a grand inquisitor, much to Joan's relief.

"Nothing," she said, "We just went in with him and stood by his side until he left."

"Both of you?" Burt looked quizzically from one to the other.

"First, Loretta asked me to watch the narcotics cabinet and I had Helen relieve me so I could see what she was doing in there," Joan explained.

"What *was* Beatty doing in there?" Burt asked more forcefully.

"He was talking to Mrs. Lipton," Joan

said. "He told her she would get well soon and that he would see her again."

"When I walked in he had the sheet pulled back and was examining her IV," Loretta said putting a sinister veil on her words. "And he jumped when I pulled the curtain back."

"It's a normal reflex," Burt conceded.

"But you said that's the way he does it," Loretta said getting excited and slapping her hand on the table.

"When did I say that?" Burt growled. Then, "Don't tell me," he blushed. He didn't want Joan to know he talked in his sleep. It was too personal, like snoring. In his own mind, Loretta's innuendo suggested he had talked about Joan in his sleep, too.

Burt opened the chart to read the history and physical exam. Dr. Pastorini had outlined Beatty's role in the patient's previous medical and surgical care. It was quite clear that Dr. Beatty had not referred the patient to Dr. Pastorini. The patient's family had insisted she come to Dr. Pastorini for a second opinion.

The seventy-four-year-old Ida Lipton had been Dr. Beatty's patient for about twenty years. Up until a year ago, her general health was good. She saw Beatty sporadically for minor illnesses and routine physical examinations. She asked him to recommend something for her increasing bouts of constipation which he did, but also strongly suggested that she have a barium enema.

A week later, Dr. Beatty called to tell her she had a lesion in her colon and stones in her gallbladder. She didn't ask him what kind of lesion, it was because she didn't want to hear that word. She couldn't ask him if it was cancer and she didn't want to hear him say it was cancer.

He was positive about the need for surgery, so for the first time in her life she was admitted to the hospital. It was comforting to have someone like Dr. Beatty as her doctor. She didn't have to explain everything all over again or try to remember any details about what brought her to the hospital. Dr. Beatty would take care of everything.

Burt continued to read. According to Dr. Pastorini, the family was told, after surgery, that Mrs. Lipton had cancer of the large bowel which had invaded the area under the liver near the gallbladder. They were told by Dr. Beatty that the cancerous colon and the gallbladder were removed but all the cancer could not be excised. His prognosis gave her six months to live. He predicted that she would become increasingly jaundiced.

He was right on that account. Within two weeks, Mrs. Lipton took on a distinctly yellow hue. It was hard to detect at first because of her almond-like complexion. Gradually, it settled into a burnt apricot color all over her skin. Except for the yellowness of her eyes, it didn't look unhealthy.

The family expected her to deteriorate rapidly after that. She surprised them as month after month she maintained her weight and, except for some pain on the right side of her abdomen, she rarely complained. No one in the family talked about the diagnosis. Everyone anticipated a painfully slow death that made any discussion taboo.

Ten months after the surgery, the family was talking openly about the situation. It started out tentatively, since no one was sure how to question such a delicate situation. It was tactless to ask why momma was still alive. She was sick with crampy pains and nausea from time to time but it was nothing like what they expected. Dr. Beatty was vague so, amidst growing dissatisfaction, the family convinced her to see another doctor.

Pastorini did every test possible and found no evidence of cancer. He called in an oncologist. Between them, they knew the tests weren't fool-proof. The persistent jaundice certainly indicated obstruction of bile flow. Taken with the history of colon surgery, it probably was due to cancer.

The obstructed bile was damaging the

liver. That was certain from the liver function tests and liver biopsy. The liver biopsy did not show any cancer. It was only a needle biopsy of the liver which could have passed between islands of cancer in the liver.

As Dr. Pastorini explained, the bile flows from the liver to the small bowel through a relatively large but delicate duct called the common bile duct. Just an inch or so before it enters the bowel, a smaller duct enters the common duct from the gallbladder which is attached like a bulbous side arm to the common duct.

The gallbladder is not essential to life, as the many people who have had it removed can attest. The way it works is known. Bile from the liver comes down the common duct. Most of it goes into the intestines. Some of it flows up into the gallbladder and is stored there. The gallbladder empties back into the common duct when it is full or when certain types of food, fats in particular, are eaten.

The wash of bile in and out of the gallbladder doesn't seem to serve any useful purpose, but the free flow of bile from the liver to the intestines is absolutely essential for two reasons. The bile contains chemicals which disperse fats, aiding digestion. Secondly, the bile contains the waste products of liver metabolism which are excreted through the bowel.

When the bile is obstructed, the back pressure on the liver eventually compromises all liver functions. It can lead to a form of cirrhosis known, aptly enough, as biliary cirrhosis. Early on, it is quite easily distinguished from alcoholic cirrhosis but in the end, the result is the same: death from liver failure.

The oncologist strongly recommended surgery for the relief of biliary obstruction to improve the liver function. If the liver could be restored, he would be able to treat Mrs. Lipton with chemotherapy. Everything depended on the liver to detoxify the poisonous chemicals he hoped would inhibit the growth of the residual cancer. It would give Mrs. Lipton three or four extra years.

There was also the problem of pain and itching. The obstruction was causing her more frequent and more severe pain. Its onset was gradual but was now accelerating. The itching came from the accumulation of bile and bile products in the skin.

Pastorini hoped to find enough length in the upper portion of the common duct free of cancer so he could attach that portion to the bowel letting the bile flow freely into the gut. It made sense to Burt who thought it was worth the chance, since she had survived this long. When he turned to the operative report, he was surprised. Under different circumstances, it would have been a pleasant surprise.

The heading itself turned his stomach sour. It read:

Pre-operative diagnosis: Cancer of the colon, metastasis with biliary obstruction.

Post-operative diagnosis: Common duct structure, No cancer seen.

Pastorini had to be pleased with himself. He not only relieved her symptoms but if his random biopsies of the area did indeed show no evidence of cancer, he saved her from dying from biliary cirrhosis. Even Beatty could come out smelling like a rose. He cured her cancer, didn't he?

Burt looked at it differently. That was all Charlie asked of him at the beginning: to look at things differently. Now he knew what Charlie meant.

Loretta and Joan were staring at him. As all the permutations and combinations went through his mind during the reading of the record, they were reflected in his face. His eyebrows rose and fell, his mouth twisted painfully, his lips moved silently in argument with an ephemeral opponent.

It was the sort of thing that often made Loretta laugh but there was nothing to laugh about now. She and Joan were waiting for him to suggest the next move. He picked up the phone from the wall and called the O.R.

"Is Dr. Pastorini scrubbed?" he asked calmly. Pause.

"Ask him to page Dr. Josephson the minute he's through. Tell him it's very urgent."

He turned back to Joan and Loretta who were still silently watching him.

"What are you two staring at?"

"What are you going to do, Burt?" Loretta asked anxiously.

"I'm not going to let him in here," Joan threatened, although she knew she didn't have that authority.

"I'm going down to talk with Jim Watson about another case and then I'll talk to Pastorini," he said matter-of-factly. "Just calm down and say nothing before you get a lynch mob started around here."

"Come on, Burt—" Loretta started to say but he stopped her.

"How's Mrs. Lipton?" he reminded her.

Loretta looked blankly at Joan. Twenty minutes had passed in which she didn't think of Mrs. Lipton once. She felt and looked guilty.

"She's okay. The other girls are watching her." Joan said.

"Let's go see."

There was no one with Mrs. Lipton but the curtain was open and other nurses could keep an eye on her from a distance, but they were busy and not privy to the information and feelings Joan and Loretta had. Burt, Joan and Loretta walked up to her bedside.

"Good morning. I'm Dr. Josephson," he smiled pleasantly.

Mrs. Lipton raised her sagging eyelids a few millimeters. It was only the first day after surgery so she was still feeling some of the after-effects of anesthesia, as well as being depressed by the Demerol.

Her long grey-black hair was combed out and lying on the pillow behind her like a zebra skin. Her skin was still yellow, a yellow that Burt could tell was fading. In the shadow of her lids, it was hard to detect any yellow. Without her false teeth, Mrs. Lipton's lips were pulled in. Lines ran up and down her lip and jaw from the retracted skin. When she tried to sit up, her left hand went out for balance; Joan and Loretta, one on each side of the bed, took her by each arm and lifted her to a sitting position. Burt watched.

Sitting up in bed, Mrs. Lipton pursed her lip and patted her cheek with her hand. She mumbled something incoherent but Joan knew what she wanted. She went to the night table and pulled out a jar containing a full set of dentures.

Mrs. Lipton waved Burt away, but not the women. She needed a little help to balance herself. One arm was restrained by the intravenous going into it and she was still weak. Burt turned to one side while Mrs. Lipton turned her head the other way and slipped the dentures neatly into her mouth. With an empty, hag-like mouth was no way to greet a stranger, especially if it was a man.

The transformation was remarkable. She knew what she was doing. Besides the pleasantness that the white row of teeth presented with her smile, it also cleared the lines around her face and made the hollowness of her cheeks disappear. She was a very pretty woman with high cheek bones and a round face. Burt would have said "good turgor" if he were thinking clinically. Even her eyes seemed brighter now that she had her teeth.

"Good morning," Mrs. Lipton said clearly but softly.

Burt didn't bother with any more formalities. It was well within the rules for a nurse to ask any doctor to check a patient she was concerned about. Burt hadn't been asked verbally but both nurses were pleased to have him check Mrs. Lipton. He pulled his stethoscope from his side pocket. It came out with several small notepapers that landed on the floor. Joan Chimento bent down to gather them up. Some had slipped under the bed. Burt held off his examination until she was out of the way.

"How do you feel today?" he asked Mrs. Lipton as Joan stood up. He didn't take the papers right away so she took the liberty to look through them.

"I got a lot of pain, Doctor." She held the right side of her abdomen. "When is Dr. Beatty coming back? He said he had something for the pain."

"For the pain in your arm?" Burt said pointing to the IV tubing.

"No, that doesn't bother me." Mrs. Lipton said as she demonstrated by moving her right arm about freely. "Here it hurts," she said pointng to the dressing over the wound.

Joan tapped him hard on the shoulder to get his attention. She was standing as straight as a rod, her heels together and her toes pointing out—something she had picked up from Loretta.

Burt turned around. She held his notes crumpled in one hand against her breast. The other hand was stretched out toward him, holding a folded piece of printed paper. Burt took it. It was a manufacturer's package insert for succinyl choline.

Burt read it, turned it over while Loretta struggled to look over his broad shoulders. She saw it and understood why Joan was biting her lip so hard.

"What are you going to do?" Loretta squeaked as Burt pocketed the piece of paper.

"I'm going to examine Mrs. Lipton, if you two don't mind," Burt said tensely. It was an important piece of evidence but he hadn't the slightest idea of what to do with it.

Burt finished his examination. Mrs. Lipton was doing fine. The two nurses followed him as he headed for the exit. He would have walked out without another word except that they were so close upon his heels he head them breathing. He stopped short.

"Where are you two going?" he glared.

"With you," Loretta said.

"I'm going to the bathroom!" he said. It was a lie but his intensity was fired by the little piece of paper in his pocket.

"You two stay here and keep an eye on Mrs. Lipton," he said less irritably. There was no way for them to object. It was their job.

"What should we do if he comes back?" Loretta asked anxiously.

"Stick to him like glue!" Burt said, and left.

THIRTEEN

There were definite similarities between the cases of Ida Lipton and Hugo Demaris but that wasn't enough for Dr. Burt Josephson to conclude that Beatty was a murderer, simply an incompetent whose surgical privileges were revoked.

Technically, they weren't revoked. Burt remembered that Charlie said he resigned without a fuss so he could continue working at Townbrook. The spectacular growth of Brady Memorial Hospital had eclipsed the Townbrook Hospital, which remained a backwater refuge for the old guard. Some new physicians had joined the staff when they first arrived in the area but once they became established almost all their patients were admitted to Brady. Bad money drives out the good and lack of standards in the hospital did the same to any qualified physician.

Burt's stomach grumbled uncomfortably. It was almost ten o'clock and he was way behind schedule. He had not yet seen one patient of his who was in the hospital. He was compulsive about making rounds early so his patients would get the benefit of a full day in the hospital. He pictured the evening and long night in the hospital as a void. Sunrise not only signaled a new day but new hope and a day closer to recovery and discharge from the hospital.

During the night, the patients slept or were supposed to sleep. No one questioned progress or lack of it during the night unless a crisis developed. Lullabies of barbiturates, narcotics and tranquilizers kept the bough from breaking. Time healed and time ravaged. Burt's morning rounds evaluated progress and relieved the suspense. Perhaps his patients were anxiously awaiting his appearance. Perhaps not. No one had paged him.

Loretta and Joan had made his present course seem more urgent than routine rounds. Discounting their insistence that Beatty had intended to harm Mrs. Lipton this morning, Burt felt that he should at least try to stop him from operating any further at Townbrook. To do this he needed some help.

Bradley and Pastorini would have to come forward, since they were directly involved. Mike Bradley had already demonstrated his reluctance to do anything openly but the death of Demaris was still troubling him. He felt responsible. Talking about it privately eased that guilt, but making it a public issue was another matter entirely. In the first place, too much time had passed and secondly, he had missed the diagnosis. Being misled by Beatty didn't seem like a viable excuse.

Joe Pastorini had been correct with Mrs. Lipton from the first time she was presented to him. Burt felt he could count on Joe if he could make him see things differently. Pastorini's report said there was no evidence of cancer which could easily be interpreted as a plus for Beatty. Damage to the common duct may have been unavoidable in a valiant attempt to remove all the cancer.

Burt's problem was to present this in the proper perspective. Charlie had to be kept out of the picture. Burt suspected that Charlie or Ed Martin had learned nothing useful from Mike Bradley other than the intuitive assessment that Bradley wasn't the killer. It was after their talk with Bradley that Charlie decided Burt was needed.

Connie Belanger's hospital record was gathering dust in some carton buried in the deepest basement of the hospital. She'd been dead for twenty years and it might not even be there, Burt was told. Yet, somehow Charlie had gotten a copy and copies of the meeting that cooked Beatty's goose at Brady Memorial Hospital. Charlie was good at some things but he had his limitations.

Dr. James Watson was the person to see. He was on the committee that had put the pressure on Beatty. In addition to remembering the circumstances, he might also have copies of his pathology reports.

Jim Watson had a twinkle in his eye that prevented his skepticism from seeming cynical. His gray hair was cut short and though thinning, there was enough to go around the top of his head. He had a long thin nose and liked to let his horn-rimmed glasses slip down to where he could look over them without bending his head. Sometimes he could look into a microscope with the glasses perched near the tip of his nose.

In his thirty years as Director of

Pathology, he enjoyed the luxury of second-guessing his colleagues in the other departments. He rarely needed to make snap judgements, could always reflect upon the specimens he received and always had the liberty of checking his answers in a book or article before committing his diagnosis to paper.

He liked surgeons better than non-surgeons the way a black-jack dealer prefers bettors to kibbitzers. When a surgeon sent him a specimen, the bets were down and the cards were dealt. Most of the time they were right and when they were wrong, intellectual dishonesty was useless. In black-jack, a player may rationalize why he hit or stood pat but it doesn't change a thing once the cards are turned over. A surgeon can make excuses but the specimen sustains the diagnosis.

A non-surgeon, an internist for instance, was like a kibbitzer. One could order a thousand tests, have them all come back normal and still claim the right thing was done. It was like asking the dealer to turn over every card in the deck without putting down a bet.

Medical technology had increased the sensitivity of laboratory tests to the point where chemical abnormalities were detectable in the absence of manifest disease. This was a double-edged sword. In some cases early detection and treatment prevented irreversible damage. In other cases, the chemical abnormality never progressed to symptoms or to organ damage which affected either the well-being or longevity of the patient.

In Jim Watson's experience, the diagnosis based on a blood test didn't always concur with his findings at autopsy. Too often there was too little correlation with the deviation of the blood test from normal and the degree of disease he found in the supposedly affected organ. And more often than not, when the opportunity to do an autopsy was presented, he found something that had been entirely unsuspected in life and more likely to have resulted in death than an abnormal test. But it was his judgment against a computer printout of a battery of laboratory tests. The result was that fewer and fewer autopsies were requested. He was trapped. He was also director of the clinical lab that produced the computer printouts.

Jim Watson was staring into a microscope at his desk so Burt knocked on the open door to get his attention. He looked up, squinted at Burt and then pushed his glasses up to the bridge of his nose.

"What are you doing here?" Dr. Watson smiled, pleasantly surprised.

They knew each other well but Burt could not remember how many times he had come to Jim's office in the last twenty years. It was not many. He walked into the long narrow office with its bookshelves and long table on one wall. Watson's desk was dominated by the binocular microscope. It was an old wooden desk, probably solid oak and scarred and stained with years of work. Next to it, end to end, was a desk of more fashionable vintage, walnut veneer with strips of chrome. It was covered with papers, reports, journals and assorted glass slides.

Watson sat in a wobbly wooden arm chair with wood slats at the back. The chair was precariously perched upon a tripod base with wheels that permitted him to slide from microscope to paperwork. The height of the seat was cranked up as high as it could go so he could look into the top of the microscope.

The seat once had a square upholstered center, undoubtedly genuine leather, but that had long been replaced by loose pillows now well flattened after years of compression.

"Sit down for awhile," Watson said as he pulled out a desk chair from the table on the opposite wall. He leaned back in his chair and put his brown loafers up on the newer desk.

"Have you been stealing from the O.R. again?" Burt asked as he sat down. It took a moment for Watson to realize he was talking about the green O.R. shirt he was wearing over his shirt and tie. He kept a stock of these shirts available rather than wear a lab coat when he worked with surgical specimens.

"I do some operating down here once in a while," he smiled.

"And your patients never complain," Burt added.

"It's too late for them when I get to operate on them," Dr. Watson grinned slyly. "Here's a case referred by one of your colleagues. According to the chart, he died of an acute myocardial infarct. I've been searching for that infarct for two days now. Grossly, there was no occlusion in any of the coronary vessels. There's nothing microscopically suggesting an early infarct. Tell me how you justify putting down he died of a coronary?"

"How long was he in the hospital?" Burt asked.

"About thirty-six hours."

"Isn't that too early for an infarct to develop?" Burt suggested.

"Should see something here after eighteen hours," Watson shook his head, "I don't know, I just don't know why this patient died."

"He must have had chest pain and EKG changes," Burt raised his eyebrows to assure Dr. Watson this had to be the case.

"Some vague chest pain and non-specific changes in the EKG," Watson smiled and waited for Burt to challenge him. Burt had no desire to pursue it further. He had something more pressing on his mind.

"The enzymes are normal also," Dr. Watson offered, "so how can he have died of an infarct?"

"I don't know but it was a good thing he was admitted," Burt said.

"Good for who?" Watson grimace. "The patient died."

"Good for his doctor who would have been sued if he wasn't admitted," Burt said.

"I'll buy that," Watson laughed. "What else are you selling today?"

"How good is your memory?" Burt began. "Do you remember a patient by the name of Connie Belanger?"

"You're damn right, I remember her!" Watson's feet hit the floor with a thud as he bolted upright. His face looked grim. "It was twenty years ago that I tried to nail that bastard Beatty!"

"Didn't you?" Burt was surprised at Watson's vehemence and swift reaction. "Didn't he get kicked out of surgery for that?"

"I would have kicked his ass all over the county," Watson sneered. Burt had never seen him look this way. "He was lucky she died. I don't think he even got sued."

"You've got some memory." Burt said appreciatively.

Jim Watson settled back in his swivel chair. "I see so much that comes through here that shouldn't, you know what I mean. I don't try to judge anybody but my feeling is that if it ain't broke, don't fix it."

Burt thought he knew what Jim meant so he nodded his agreement, but he was more interested in specifics than philosophy at this point. Jim Watson stopped talking as if the subject was closed. Burt waited but the pathologist only stared at his own fingernails as he cleaned some dirt from them. His eyebrows knitted in a troubled, introverted stare. He completely ignored Burt.

"What happened twenty years ago?" Burt asked after a moment.

"Well, you know what happened," Watson said giving him a disturbing look. "You were here!"

"No, I came just after that," Burt said innocently.

"You know he stripped out an artery instead of a vein. That girl would have lost her leg, but she died. By the time it came before the Executive Committee she was already dead and gone. Everyone was for taking away his surgical privileges. That was no problem. Some of those guys would take anyone's privileges away just so there would be more for them to do. I wanted to have his license pulled but that was too much trouble for the rest of them. They were worried all the publicity would give the hospital a bad name. And since she was dead, everyone felt it was past history."

The twinkle in his eyes was gradually restored as he spoke. He was no longer intense or angry but philosophic and reflective about what must have seemed like ancient history. Burt had tapped two distinct memories. One was personal, angry and spontaneous. The other was deliberative and perhaps tempered, refined and justified over a period of twenty years.

"He still operates at Townbrook," Burt said, probing with the hope of stirring some resentment. Watson had aroused his own resentment. There was no doubt now in his mind that Beatty was a rotten apple but he couldn't bring himself to accuse Beatty of murder.

"That's none of my business, thank God," Watson shrugged. "I don't know where he gets his patients or what he does over there."

"Some of his mistakes end up here," Burt said as he fingered the package insert in his side pocket.

"Not that I know of," Watson looked surprised but was there a defensive overtone to his words. "I only know what those monkeys upstairs tell me," he said referring to the surgeons in the O.R.

"He referred a patient to Mike Bradley about three months ago. Hugo Demaris,"

Burt said.

"Demaris?" Watson said as if he were thinking out loud. "I just got a culture report back from the state lab," he leaned over the "new" desk stacked with papers. He rummaged through them and came up with a single sheet.

"Here it is," he read it aloud. It had been delivered six weeks ago. A copy had been sent to Bradley but Watson's copy hadn't been filed yet.

"The culture was positive but we knew that from the biopsy he sent down," Watson said flatly. "Bradley screwed up on this one. I heard he developed a fistula."

"And an M.I. which killed him," Burt added. He regretted that conclusion but it seemed to come out automatically as conventional wisdom.

"What about that biopsy he sent you with the silk sutures in it?" Burt asked.

"That was a tuberculous granuloma in fat and connective tissue," Watson said.

"What about the silk sutures?" Burt prodded eagerly.

"I don't know where they came from," Watson shrugged, "but they had been there for a while. There weren't fresh."

"Beatty put them there," Burt stated.

"Beatty?" Watson's voice was raised in disbelief.

"Yeah," Burt said confidently, "he did an appendectomy which turned sour post-operatively. It turned out to be an obstructed right ureter.''

"I didn't know that." Watson said soberly as his eyebrows came together in a frown.

"And there's another case of Beatty's that Pastorini operated on a few days ago,'' Burt kept his voice conspiratorially low. "Ida Lipton. Obstructive jaundice with a history of colon cancer.''

"I just read her slides. Here they are." Watson picked several glass slides from a cardboard compartment beside his microscope. "There's no cancer in the specimen he sent me.''

Burt declined the offer to look at the slides through the microscope. Was it possible Beatty had actually cured this patient of cancer? Most surgeons think they do excise all the cancer; at least that's what they set out to do. If there is any possibility that they were successful, they tell that to the patient with guarded optimism.

A surgeon might be over-optimistic and present the patient with hope. Beatty had told the Liptons there was no hope, which meant he had left behind a visible amount of cancer. Pastorini had found no evidence of cancer.

"That doesn't mean anything," Watson said. "Sometimes what they take out is less important than what they leave in.''

"Were you ever curious about why Connie Belanger died?'' Burt asked hesitantly.

"Sure!'' Watson said and gave Burt a queer look. "I'm interested in why every patient dies. Why are you after Beatty?'' he asked quietly.

Burt felt a little short of breath. True, he was after Beatty, but he had been trying hard to be subtle about it. At least, he thought he was being subtle. He never said he was after Beatty and felt uncomfortable about the label. Beatty could sue him if he could prove malice and "being after'' someone sounded malicious.

"Hugo Demaris was a cousin of a friend of a friend,'' Burt said and added, "of another friend,'' so Watson would certainly know he was lying about the reason for his interest. It freed Watson of the taint of conspiracy.

"I understand,'' Watson smiled. "He's a slippery little bastard and will tell the family anything. I tried to get a post on Belanger myself, but somehow he got to the family first. What could I do?''

"This cousin of Demaris doesn't like Beatty. He hates him, as a matter of fact. Thinks he's crazy. He thinks Beatty slipped in here and killed his cousin Hugo Demaris,'' Burt recited.

"And did your friend also tell you about Connie Belanger?'' Watson asked. "Is this friend of yours a reporter named Charlie Dresden?''

Burt flushed feverishly. His cheeks puffed out, his eyes squinted tightly and he slowly let the air out of his cheeks. He was furious that Charlie never told him he had spoken with Watson. He was embarrassed by the revelation.

"I wouldn't trust him further than I could throw you!" Watson said irritably. "He sat right there giving me the third degree for an hour. Why didn't I isolate Demaris if he had TB? What rules there are for accepting transfer patients from another hospital? Why didn't I get a post on Demaris? I don't order post-mortems!" Watson cried, exasperated. "Then he started in on Belanger! God, that was twenty years ago. He's out to make a big stink. I don't know why, either. He could go to any hospital in the country and ask a lot of questions to make anyone look bad."

"Did he say why he was asking all these questions?" Burt asked, hoping he had. It would save him from looking foolish.

"Hell, no!" Watson almost shouted. He controlled his voice and his emotions. "He started in just the way you did. I went along and answered his questions for a while and then I got suspicious. He wouldn't tell me why he was asking all these questions. Insisted he needed all the answers before he could tell me. But I see he got to you. I was waiting for you tell me! What's he up to?" Watson finished angrily.

Burt was saved by the page. The operator paged him to call 271. It was Joe Pastorini calling as requested. Burt asked him to come down to Watson's office. In the meantime, Burt's answer to Watson's question would have to wait. He wasn't absolutely sure what Charlie was up to, anyway.

Although Charlie hadn't told him everything, Burt had to agree Beatty had done some terrible things. The way he saw it now, Charlie had tried to dope out this story using his usual resources. It ran pretty deep but there were a lot of things Charlie either didn't understand or, more likely, couldn't corroborate. After all, he could have gotten any physician to explain the record to him or supply him with innuendo, probabilities or whatever was necessary.

He needed some personal witnesses. Apparently, the direct approach with Watson had turned sour. Watson, correctly, or incorrectly, didn't trust Charlie. Bradley was sincere but vague; he was too personally involved. Charlie's approach now made sense to Burt.

After being rebuffed by Watson, Charlie needed someone to act as a liaison between him and the medical establishment. It had to be someone who was knowledgeable, respected and neutral as far as Beatty was concerned. Someone who would have nothing to lose if Beatty was exposed.

Charlie had copies of the hospital records

and evidence that Beatty had possession of succinyl choline. He didn't have anyone who would testify Beatty had used it. He needed more than a liaison. He needed someone who would become a partisan; someone who would believe as he did in Beatty's guilt.

Burt appreciated Charlie's problem more clearly. He had seen it in Jim Watson's reaction. Watson was certainly no friend of Beatty's. From what Watson just said, it was probably his actions more than any other's that got Beatty banned from Brady Memorial. And he was willing to go further until he was overruled on the Executive Committee. That was twenty years ago.

Burt's perspective was quite different. This wasn't malpractice anymore. It was murder and Charlie's problem was that he made the two inseparable. There was no place to take this double-headed charge. There wasn't enough evidence to take to a grand jury or the police and it was too heavy to present to a medical board.

Obviously, Charlie had discussed the Belanger case and the Demaris case with Watson. Watson had let him go on about Demaris but got ticked off when it came to Belanger. Perhaps Charlie had hit a raw nerve, some guilty feelings Jim still had about Connie Belanger. Perhaps he had sounded threatening. If he didn't come right out and accuse Beatty of murder, it could sound threatening to Watson.

Perspective was everything. Charlie had probably doled out as little information as he could while trying to get Watson to talk about the Belanger case. It looked like Charlie was trying to stir up a lot of dirt. Burt believed Watson would have been more cooperative if Charlie had told him he was investigating a possible murder. He might not believe him but he wouldn't have thrown him out of the office.

Watson knew more than anyone about Belanger and Demaris except for Beatty. Burt couldn't judge the impact of the Belanger case because he didn't know enough about it. The Demaris case had aroused his interest but didn't convince him of anything. It was Ida Lipton who had made him a solid supporter of Charlie Dresden. Burt's credibility with Watson had been hurt because of Charlie's intervention. Fortunately, Joe Pastorini arrived to present Ida Lipton's case for him. Once Watson and Pastorini were convinced, Bradley would have to go along with them.

Burt greeted Dr. Pastorini in the hallway outside the pathology office. He quickly ushered him into Dr. Watson's office. Joe Pastorini hadn't bothered to change his O.R. greens. His muscular arms stuck out of the almost sleeveless shirt. They weren't made sleeveless but his broad shoulders pulled the sleeves up and made it tight under his arms.

"Sit right down here," Burt directed Joe, "and tell this doctor about Ida Lipton."

Dr. Pastorini looked at Burt bewildered and distressed by the directive.

"Go on, tell him!" Burt insisted.

"What have you got to do with Ida Lipton?" Pastorini demanded indignantly.

"Nothing," Burt said with his arms folded standing high above the seated Pastorini. "Have I ever discussed this case with you before? Even one word?"

"No," Pastorini shrugged, raised his eyebrows at Watson as if Burt was crazy. "What do you want to know?"

"Just present the case," Burt instructed him.

"What did you find on those biopsies?" he asked Watson instead of following Burt's orders.

"Never mind what he found," Burt interrupted strongly, "tell us what you found!"

"I found a strictured common bile duct and I fixed it." Pastorini said proudly. "And if I get my hands on that bastard Beatty I'm gonna cut his balls off. He is such a liar! There was nothing in that specimen, right? He never did a bowel resection. He's an out and out liar," Pastorini looked around to see if anyone heard. Only Burt and Jim Watson were there and the door was closed.

"That poor woman never had a bowel

cancer!'' he continued, earnest but more subdued. "He screwed up her common duct when he took out the gallbladder. He knew he did. That's why he told her she'd be jaundiced. That's why he told her she would die—and he was going to let her die!''

"Is that what this is all about?" he asked looking from Burt to Jim. Dr. Watson sat silently rubbing his hand across his chin while Joe was talking. He offered nothing now. Burt was waiting for his reaction.

"Where do you fit into this?" he asked Burt.

"Tell him about Connie Belanger," Burt said to Jim Watson.

Watson made a sour face and turned away from both of them. Pastorini looked confused but unconcerned. He didn't like riddles. If Jim didn't want to answer it was okay with him. He had another case waiting upstairs.

"Belanger was a patient Beatty operated on twenty years ago," Burt began, looking straight at Pastorini. He was determined to get it all out but Watson slapped the top of his desk so hard that Pastorini literally twitched in his seat.

"That's ancient history," Watson said in a soft but tough voice. "It's well established that Beatty is a lousy surgeon. What the hell is your reporter friend going to do with this information now? What do you hope to gain by hanging this dirty linen in a newspaper?''

"What newspaper?" Pastorini said sharing Watson's feelings most emphatically.

"Forget the newspaper!" Burt exclaimed. "I want Joe to hear this because it might save Mrs. Lipton's life. It's not so ancient history if it keeps repeating itself. Belanger was just the beginning as far as we know. That was the case that got Beatty kicked out of here. He stripped an artery instead of a vein. The patient died from undetermined causes. Is that a fair summary?" he looked at Watson for a challenge. Watson shook his head disgustedly. It was hard to tell if he was reacting to the story or the fact that Burt was telling it.

"About three months ago," Burt continued, "Beatty did an appendectomy on a patient named Demaris. It turned out that this patient had renal TB with an obstructed ureter. He sent him over to Bradley without telling him about the TB. Bradley operated and the patient developed a fistula. Two weeks later the patient died."

"You forgot to say the patient had a heart attack," Watson said angrily but keeping his tone quiet.

"Okay, okay," Pastorini said rapidly as he held up his hand for order. It was merely a hint of discord between Burt and Jim that he wanted to stop before it blew up. "As I see the problem, the only thing we can do is to present my case with the Demaris case to the administration at Townbrook. I agree Beatty shouldn't be allowed to do surgery anywhere."

"What if they don't cooperate?" Jim Watson asked. "I don't think they will listen to you attacking one of their most active doctors. He keeps that hospital filled. Are you going to take his place there? In a pig's eye!"

"Call the record room at Townbrook and see how he signed her out," Pastorini suggested to Watson. Watson picked up the phone immediately.

Burt sat down on the long table which bowed downward under his weight. He looked anxiously at his wristwatch and thought about the patients waiting for him. This was important and he couldn't rush it. The process of discovery had convinced him as much as the facts themselves. Words alone were subject to many interpretations.

"What do you expect to find out from Townbrook?" he quietly asked Pastorini while Watson was on the phone.

"If he signed her out as a colectomy, I think we got him," Pastorini smiled. "I'll swear there was no colectomy and they won't be able to come up with a specimen in pathology. He told the patient and her family he did a colectomy. If he billed for a colectomy, then it's fraud.

233

"You think she had all her problems just from having her gallbladder out?" Burt was a little queasy as he unconsciously patted his abdomen on the right side.

"Oh, easily," Pastorini was unaware of Burt's personal interest in gallbladder surgery. "It's an inch or less between the cystic duct and the common duct. With the blood vessels there, if you get bleeding and you fuck up like Beatty, it's easy to clamp the common duct. Then a stricture develops and it can be a horrible mess. I don't think he cut it because she didn't have a fistula, which is why she didn't die."

Burt closed his eyes tightly as he mentally dismissed Nate Simon's distant diagnosis. No gallbladder surgery for him, even with someone as good as Pastorini.

"He signed her out as cholecystitis and cholecystectomy," Watson announced as he put down the phone.

"That's not what he told the family," Pastorini sighed, taking a deep breath. "In that case, it's up to the family."

"Who's going to tell them?" Burt asked.

"I will," Pastorini assured him, 'as soon as she's well enough,"

"When will that be?" Burt asked suspecting he was holding a kicker.

"In six to eight weeks," Pastorini said quite pleasantly. He saw no urgency in the matter.

"Why not right now?" Burt urged him.

"Because I want to be sure she's completely healed without any complications," Pastorini insisted. "The upshot of this will certainly be a lawsuit and when a lawyer gets a hold of it everyone's going to be named. Including me!"

"Why should you be sued?" Burt asked.

"I won't be," Joe said positively, "but if she develops a fistula, even if it's not my fault, a lawyer leaves that to the courts."

"Even if you're not sued," Watson chimed in smiling, "you'll still have to appear in court for the patient."

A cloud passed over Pastorini's face. He thought about the possibility and the time involved. Burt was thinking the same thing and he could read Pastorini's thoughts from the look on his face.

"There's more than malpractice involved here," Burt said standing up. There wasn't much space in the long narrow room. He walked behind Watson who didn't turn his chair around. Burt was isolated on the far side of the room. Pastorini looked at him but Burt didn't want to talk to Watson's back. He came back to his perch on the table.

"There are two cases in which Beatty screwed up and two cases in which there were unexpected deaths. I don't think that's a coincidence and I don't think those patients died of complications. They are deliberate deaths and Beatty is responsible."

Pastorini and Watson stared at each other and then at Burt in disbelief. Watson's glasses were at the tip of his nose as he squinted over them toward Burt. Burt took a deep breath and went on.

"He won't tell me the details of the Belanger case but you have to concede this much," he spoke to Watson. "If she had lived as an amputee, Beatty's neck would be in the noose, even now."

Watson crossed his legs and covered his mouth with his hand. He said nothing and hid his feelings very well. He made no move to deny Burt.

"So it was to Beatty's advantage she died. A similar series of events put Demaris in the same situation with regard to Beatty and he ended up dead unexpectedly. I know he had a heart attack," Burt raised his hand to stop Watson from saying the same thing, "but it was a mild one and he should have survived. One thing neither of you know is that he pulled the same thing with the Demaris family that he did with the Liptons. He told them he had cancer and was expected to die. Bradley will testify to that."

"Either you're crazy or Beatty's crazy," Pastorini interrupted. This seemed to dismiss the possibility of deliberate death.

"I'm not crazy," Burt said too defensively. "Beatty was the last person to see Demaris alive."

236

"How do you know that?" Watson asked doubtfully.

"A nurse in the ICU saw him," Burt said then waited to let the fact sink in. There was no rebuttal. "Beatty was in the ICU this morning. I saw him coming out myself." Burt hesitated here as he thought about Loretta's and Joan's reaction. It seemed like the sort of thing that might make him sound less convincing if he told it exactly as it happened.

"I discussed this with Loretta last night,' he said. "She's working in the ICU. She saw Beatty go in to Mrs. Lipton."

"What's wrong with that?" Pastorini asked. "I'd visit a patient I once operated on. Wait a minute!" he said anxiously and horrified, "What's happened to Mrs. Lipton?"

"Nothing, she's fine," Burt assured him. "Loretta went in with him. As soon as she came in, he ran out. And we found this package insert under the bed after he left." Burt handed the piece of paper to Pastorini.

"Where did you get this from?" Pastorini asked as he read the folded insert.

"I found it under Mrs. Lipton's bed." Burt hoped they would see the connection.

"So what does this prove?" Pastorini asked as he handed the paper to Watson.

"Beatty must have dropped it when he was in there. Don't you get it?" Burt sounded desperate. "He planned to use it on Mrs. Lipton.''

"That's rididculous!" Pastorini said. "Why should he harm Mrs. Lipton? She's getting better. He's going to be a hero to her.''

"Don't you see the connection?" Burt pleaded. "Demaris was getting better. Belanger would have survived. If Lipton survives, Beatty will be sued.''

"That's all speculation," Pastorini insisted. "If I don't say anything to the family, Beatty isn't even threatened.''

"But you said you would," Burt countered.

"I said I might," Pastorini corrected him. "And that's up to me. I don't know what right you have to be involved.''

"I have every right to be involved," Burt said indignantly, but he was clearly hurt by the challenge. "And what right do you have to put me down that way?''

"You find a piece of paper under a bed and you accuse Beatty of murder," Pastorini said disparagingly. "Anyone could have dropped it. I'm sure one the anesthesiologists made rounds this morning. One of them could have dropped it!''

"Hold on a minute," Jim Watson held up his hand and sat upright. "Let's not get too personal about this. I think Burt's head was filled with a lot of nonsense by some newspaper reporter," he spoke directly at

Joe Pastorini. Then to Burt he said, "Am I right?"

"It's not nonsense," Burt said feeling trapped again.

"He was after something," Jim insisted, "and I don't know what he told you, but he didn't fool me."

"He wasn't trying to fool you," Burt said bitterly.

"Where'd you get the idea Beatty was trying to kill anyone with this?" Watson asked thrusting the slip of paper toward Burt.

"He found some of these plus a vial of succinyl choline in Beatty's locker at Townbrook," Burt took the paper from Watson.

"How'd he get into Beatty's locker?" Watson demanded.

"What difference does it make?" Burt countered. "What was this stuff doing in there?"

"I think we're just going around in circles," Watson said taking off his glasses. He had thick crowfeet under his eyes and looked much older than usual as he stared at Burt. "I don't want anything to do with him. He's out to smear a lot of people!"

Joe Pastorini squirmed uncomfortably in his seat. He avoided Burt who was looking to him for some kind of support.

"I gotta go," Pastorini said, deliberately looking at his watch rather than Burt. He just got up and left.

"I'd be careful, Burt, or this guy will leave you holding the bag," Dr. James Watson warned.

FOURTEEN

Burt finally got started on his morning rounds close to eleven o'clock. If anyone noticed he was late, they didn't mention it. Maybe it was because Dr. Josephson hurried through his visits and examinations. He seemed preoccupied. Three times, on different floors, he had to be reminded to renew medications.

It was only an administrative detail. The nurse would have continued the medication anyway, but the rules required that the doctor reorder every three days. Without this rule, some patients would get medication long after it was useful.

A few nurses noticed Dr. Josephson talking to himself. His muttering was too soft to be heard but it was accompanied by fierce changes of facial expression which made one nurse laugh out loud.

Burt was now more sure than ever that Beatty was responsible for Demaris' death. He had the means and the opportunity—and now Burt realized what the motive was. It was crazy, but self-preservation and greed are strong motivators.

Watson and Pastorini had made him see the motive he had not been able to figure out before. They didn't deny it was possible or refuse to believe what Burt had said about Demaris. Watson knew about Belanger personally and Pastorini was ready to pull Beatty down on Lipton. Watson's only argument was against Charlie and it gave Pastorini second thoughts.

Burt thought his subtleties had been effective. Bradley poured out his heart and Burt waited before he lifted the veil from Bradley's guilt. Watson was open and full of vinegar. Pastorini provided the active link that gave urgency to the conclusion.

Either the recipe was incomplete or the

parts weren't added in the right order. As Burt heard the story unfold, first from Bradley, then from Watson and finally Pastorini, he was sure Beatty's goose was cooked. But Charlie had greased the pan for him. It was scorched for Watson and left unoiled for Bradley and Pastorini. Something was needed to stir the pot, a catalyst to bring it to a boil.

Burt hurried to his office. He was behind schedule and there was another urgent matter; the grumbling of his stomach reminding him he had missed lunch. It was just as well, since he resolved to start a new diet. He denied to himself that Mrs. Lipton's complications from gallbladder surgery had anything to do with his decision.

He dashed past Karen Eberle, who followed him to his private office. There were five patients in his waiting room and he was late. He expected some smart-ass remarks from her about his responsibilities or how tired she was of lying for him when he was late.

"Not now, Karen," he waved her off. "I've got an important call to make. Just go back there and take some temperatures or something."

"They're all done!" Karen said in a huff. "I just wanted to tell you that I'll be able to work tonight."

"Tonight?" Burt was puzzled for a moment. "That's right, we switched. It's okay,

Karen. Loretta said she would come in.''

''I really don't mind,'' Karen insisted.

Burt thought about it for a few seconds, then said, ''I promised her. It wouldn't be fair to disappoint her. Now get out of here!''

A few minutes passed while he composed his thoughts. While he could lie easily enough to serve his ego, deceit was a new experience for him. When he felt ready, he called Emery Beatty.

''This is Melvin Lipton,'' he said in the deepest possible voice he could manage. ''I'm calling about Ida Lipton, she's a patient of Dr. Beatty.''

Beatty's nurse asked him to hold on. He wondered if the handkerchief over the phone changed his voice at all. It was something he had seen in the movies. His own voice was familiar enough to arouse suspicion. Beatty spoke to him.

''I'm calling about my aunt, Ida Lipton,'' Burt said.

''She's no longer my patient,'' Dr. Beatty said curtly.

''I know, but I wanted to call and thank you for what you did for her,'' Burt said to keep him interested by the flattery. ''I don't think it was right for my cousins to take Aunt Ida to another doctor when she liked you so much. I told them you did the best for her.''

''Of course I did. What's the point of all

this?'' he asked arrogantly. He spoke so loudly that Burt had to hold the phone away from his ear.

"Dr. Pastorini told them Aunt Ida didn't have cancer. They are really strange, that family. I was overjoyed but they got all upset. They said she never had cancer. I think that is the height of perversity. I told them you saved Aunt Ida's life by removing all the cancer. Now, isn't that right?''

"Absolutely! Absolutely!'' Beatty shouted. "Where did they ever get such nonsense? I wish it were so.'' he said calming down. "It's hard to face the truth and even harder for some doctors to tell the truth. Believe me, I wish I were wrong. It would be a miracle if she didn't have cancer.''

"I feel awful now,'' Burt said. "What can I say to them? I believed Dr. Pastorini but I told them it was you who cured her of cancer. Now you say it isn't so?'' Burt pleaded.

"It's possible! It's possible,'' Beatty said, thinking it over. "Why are they so upset if they think she has no cancer?''

"They say she never had cancer to begin with.'' Burt bit his lower lip nervously.

"That's ridiculous! A lie. An out and out lie,'' Beatty went on sucking in air so it could be heard over the phone. "Time will tell. I mean—I pray to God she doesn't. It's out of my hands now, anyway.''

"What should I do, Dr. Beatty?" Burt asked.

"Pray for her!" Beatty said softly and hung up.

Burt stared into the buzzing phone until it became silent. The way Beatty said, "Pray for her" startled him. It also gave him a chill at the back of his neck. He wasn't sure he had done the right thing. As long as Ida Lipton stayed in the ICU, it was a safe plan. Burt decided to call Loretta.

"Mrs. Josephson, please," he said when he got through the switchboard to the ICU clerk.

"Hi," he said pleasantly, keeping his main concern hidden. "You're coming to the office this afternoon. Just wanted to remind you."

"What time?" Loretta asked.

"About five is okay. How's Mrs. Lipton?"

"Fine, she's sitting up in a chair," Loretta said. "Joe Pastorini was in to see her. He asked me about Dr. Beatty. I just said that he was in to see her. Was that okay?"

"Is that all you told him?" Burt asked disappointedly. He didn't know quite how to ask the question. He wanted her to tell everything.

"Of course it was!" Loretta said indignantly. "After you growled like a bear and said in front of Joan I was hysterical, I wouldn't say a word of it to anyone. What's the matter, Burt? Did you talk to Joe about Mrs. Lipton?"

"I did," Burt sighed. "He knows Beatty is a bum but that's as far as he will go. I laid it all out for him, told him everything, but he won't buy the possibility that Beatty is trying to kill Mrs. Lipton. It's hard to believe anyone, much less a physician, can deliberately kill. Maybe he's crazy. I could be wrong. Pastorini and Watson think I am."

"What should we do?" Loretta asked.

"Just keep an eye on Mrs. Lipton. I'll see you later."

FIFTEEN

Loretta came to the office wearing her uniform, a white pant suit. It was all white but distinctly styled with a fold and embroidered designs around the collar and neck. Karen Eberle greeted her with mixed emotions but put on a cheerful front. Despite Loretta's protestations, she was still a possible replacement for Karen. No matter what, the boss's wife always had the last word.

So Karen insisted she would go out and bring back their supper. It made things much easier. Burt was behind schedule all day so the evening was heavier than usual. It took him less than twenty minutes to down his large hero sandwich and half of Loretta's.

The last patient left at nine-thirty. Burt finished making some notes and tidied up the stack of medical records on his desk. He picked up a dozen folders and carried them to Loretta who looked exhausted from working the double shift, first at the hospital and then at the office.

"What is this?" Burt asked opening the top folder in his hands.

"What Burt? What?" Loretta's hands covered her eyes.

"This paragraph you wrote on Mr. Golomb's record," Burt reproached.

"Let me see that." Loretta took the folder from him.

"In the first place, I know he's an alcoholic. He's been coming to me for twenty years. If you look through the chart, I've noted it several times. In the second place, he'll never go for psychiatric counseling or A.A. or anything. He'd lose his job if anyone found out. And in the third place, you're littering up my records."

"I'm sorry. I just thought it would be a

good idea if he knew about these places," Loretta apologized.

"And what about this?" he asked, opening the next folder. "Who asked you to give birth control advice to Susan Miller? I hardly know her. She just came in for a physical exam for college."

"If she's going to college, don't you think it's a good idea for her to know about birth control?" Loretta defended herself.

"Let her mother tell her! And knowing her mother, I'm surprised she let her go to a coed college," Burt said indifferently.

"That's the point!" Loretta replied aggressively. "You couldn't tell her and I felt it was my responsibility. She was very grateful."

"I bet," Burt sighed. "But don't put it in the chart. If she goes home and tells her mother I can say she learned it in the street. Besides, why is it your responsibility? You're just supposed to get their names, weigh them and take blood pressures. Look at this one," reading from her note. " 'Mrs Cohen is a 68-year-old obese diabetic who could easily be controlled without insulin if she would adhere to her diet and lose at least forty pounds. There is also an occasional irregular heartbeat, probably due to a sinus arrhythmia, but an EKG is indicated to rule out premature ventricular contractions.' "

"What's wrong with that?"

"You're not the doctor. I'm the doctor," Burt said, exasperated. "See the sign on the door? It says, 'Burt Josephson, M.D.' That's who they come to see."

"This is the way it's done, Burt!" Loretta said warmly. "That's the new way! The nurses in the ICU record their own histories and physical exams and set out a plan for the patient to supplement and aid the physician."

Burt snapped the folder shut.

"You're absolutely correct. File these!" he said placing them on her desk. He turned quickly and walked down the corridor steaming.

"File them yourself!" she called after him.

"Leave them for Karen," he sounded tired. He came back to her and leaned in the doorway.

"Wanna fool around on my examining table?" he leered at her.

"No, thank you!" she said curtly. "I'm tired and have to get up early for work."

"You worked very hard today and were perfect," he said softly. "Everything you wrote down was correct. I just don't have time for some of those things unless the patient is really interested."

"I know," she said. "You look very tired, too. Can we go home now?"

"As soon as I call the hospital to check on Mrs. Lipton," he said.

When the nurse in the ICU told him that Mrs. Lipton had been transferred to a private room, Burt felt sick to his stomach. It started as a faint quiver and progressed to a stabbing pain under his ribs. He felt cold and nauseated. He could barely ask, "Why?"

The explanation was quite straightforward. Mrs. Lipton was in the Unit "on priority" which meant the opposite of what it sounded like. The Unit was full and she had the lowest priority. If anyone came to the hospital with a heart attack or anything requiring intensive care, she was cleared for transfer to make room for the new patient.

Burt slumped in his chair, regretting he had made that irritating call to Emery Beatty. He saw it as a fool's gambit. In the ICU under close supervision, Mrs. Lipton was perfectly safe. Beatty knew this unless he was totally psychotic. In a private room, Burt had risked her life without her consent.

Loretta, wondering why he was taking so long, came to get him.

"You look terrible," she said quite worried. "Are you all right?"

His skin was blanched. With heavy eyes and a face sadder than a hound dog, he looked up at her.

"She's been transferred to a private room," he said, swallowing hard.

"Yes, she was on priority," Loretta said calmly. "She's fine. There was no reason to keep her there."

"I thought she'd stay there three or four days."

"Why? The surgery went real well. She's alert and sitting up. She doesn't need constant nursing care," Loretta said.

"What about Beatty?" Burt said tensely.

"Since you weren't very impressed with the way Joan and I reacted this morning, we decided it would be okay to put her on priority. Besides, I probably scared him off for good."

"You should have told me that," Burt said holding his head and sitting way back in his chair. "After I finished talking to Watson and Pastorini, I was convinced Beatty was guilty. Guilty of trying to poison Mrs. Lipton and a few others. I almost had Pastorini convinced but he chickened out in the end. He's going to sit on this unless something drastic happens to change his mind."

"Nothing drastic is going to happen to Mrs. Lipton," Loretta assured him. "If Beatty wants to save his skin, he's better off staying away from her."

"I hope you're right," Burt sighed.

"Why shouldn't I be right?" Loretta said confidently. "Only a raving lunatic would try anything now. He knew I was watching him."

"Oh, shit!" Burt cried out.

"Oh, shit, what?" Loretta countered immediately. "You've certainly changed your tune! What was I supposed to think after you left this morning?"

"It's not your fault. It's all mine," Burt said sadly. "I called Beatty this afternoon and told him what Pastorini found at surgery."

"That's good for Mrs. Lipton. He knows that you know," she paused to itemize with her fingers, "and Pastorini knows. He wouldn't dare try anything now."

"He doesn't know it was me," Burt said. "It doesn't matter if he is a lunatic, which he has to be if he's done these things. It's crazy but there's a definite pattern. He's gotten away with it before. He doesn't care if other doctors know he's a lousy surgeon. A dead patient makes it a dead issue. Even if it's not true, if his twisted mind thinks it's true, he will act on that premise."

"If that's the case, Burt, then I'll sit with her tonight."

"You're going to sit with her and then work tomorrow after working sixteen hours today?" Burt said dubiously. "Forget it. I'll get someone from the registry. But damn it! I'm not really certain," he said slamming his fist down on the desk.

"It's Charlie Dresden's fault!" he went on. "Okay, so Beatty is a menace in the operating rom. Everyone agrees. But no one will go so far as to even think Beatty would kill someone deliberately. They know the same things I do. The only difference is they haven't been seduced by Charlie Dresden."

"Burt, I hate to see you so upset," Loretta pleaded. "Call Charlie and see what he thinks. Maybe you're right. Maybe he was just trying to turn you on to this madness. Level with him and tell him you're scared for Mrs. Lipton's sake."

Burt was willing to try anything. Running into the hosptial to provide Mrs. Lipton with protection could prove embarrassing. He didn't mind paying for the special-duty nurses but his explanation would seem ludicrous if he couldn't prove anything. Pastorini had given him a taste of that this afternoon. Ironically, he feared, he could be handcuffed instead of Beatty.

Charlie wasn't at his office. Burt made it sound like an emergency and was told he would be called back right away. It took about ten minutes. Loretta was too tired to protest Burt's suggestions, which were going off on tangents. She sat silently with him until the phone rang.

"Charlie, this thing is driving me silly," Burt said forcefully. "You have to lay everything out on the table for me. I believe you but I need tangible proof about Beatty.

I did a terrible thing today. I hope it turns out to be a silly prank. Nevertheless, I knowingly put some unsuspecting woman in jeopardy. Let me tell you . . . ,"

"I know all about it," Charlie interrupted. "Emery Beatty called me this afternoon and accused me of pretending to be Mrs. Lipton's nephew. He said I was harassing him and theatened me with a court order to stop."

"But what about Mrs. Lipton?" Burt pressed anxiously. "She's not in the ICU anymore. Beatty will try to get at her."

"No he won't," Charlie said positively. "I figured it was you and told him so. He screamed about conspiracy and shit like that. I told him to go ahead and sue me. I dared him to but he knew I had the story on Demaris and probably a few other things. Unfortunately, I think I scared him off."

"What do you mean?" Burt growled. "It's a good thing you did."

"Unfortunately, I told him that if anything happened to Mrs. Lipton, even if he had nothing to do with it, I would hold him personally responsible. I lost my head in the heat of the argument. He said he was leaving town until she left the hospital. I'm sorry, Burt. It was a great idea but I screwed it up for you."

"Jesus!" Burt bellowed with relief. "Charlie, that's good news. It washes my hands of this whole thing. Don't get me wrong. I think there will be some effort to stop Beatty from operating at Townbrook but unless you have some solid evidence, from now on you're on your own.''

"We're going to wrap it up here,'' Charlie said indifferently. "My editor thinks we've spent too much time on this already. He wants something to print.''

"What do you mean?'' Burt asked.

"He wants a story after we spent all this time investigating. That's how I earn my money.''

"What kind of story do you have?'' Burt wondered.

"I just started writing,'' Charlie said. "The piece is called, 'Death Row In The Hospital—The Mortality Files of Dr. X.' ''

SIXTEEN

Three weeks later, Mrs. Lipton was discharged from the hospital. She recovered from surgery, but it would take another three weeks at home with the tube in her common duct before that part was safely healed.

Burt never kept the tennis date with Pastorini. Their relationship, while not broken, was considerably cooler. Burt felt betrayed by his failure to act on the matter of Dr. Beatty. Pastorini said, "Burt Josephson was pissing against the wind."

The most visible change in Burt's life had nothing to do with Beatty or Pastorini. He began his hospital rounds, as usual, in the ICU, but now he came in at noon.

"Good morning," he greeted Joan Chimento who was bent over the conference room table writing out schedules for the coming month.

""Good morning," Joan said without looking up. She recognized the voice and could feel his huge presence, "Oh, my God," she looked up, "it's lunchtime already!"

Burt went over to the large percolator coffee urn. He placed a styrofoam cup under the spigot. A few oily drops of black liquid dropped into the cup.

"Don't drink that," Joan warned him. "I'm just going to make a small pot. Sit down for a minute."

Burt sat.

"Don't make any on my account," he said. "I'll go down to the coffee shop and have some breakfast."

"Breakfast?" Joan laughed. "That was six hours ago."

"Only farmers have to get up with the sunrise," Burt said. "There are twenty-four hours in a day and one part of the day is as good as the other for my work. It's more convenient for my patients also. I have daily office hours now from four to ten at night. A lot of people who work can come in to see me without taking time off. Then I pick up Loretta from work and go to supper."

"How does she like working?" Joan asked as she plugged in the small coffee percolator.

"She loves it," Burt said. "And I don't think she'll change to days. Three to eleven is working out okay."

"Your friend, Charlie Dresden, is doing some job on Dr. Beatty," Joan said. "Everyone around here knows he's Dr. X. Townbrook is in a panic. Three patients were transferred here yesterday."

Burt sniffed and turned away.

"What's the matter?" Joan said as she sat down opposite him. "Do you think he's lying?"

"I don't recognize anyone in his articles," Burt said, annoyed at the subject. "He mentions Townbrook Hospital by name several times but other than that it could be anywhere."

"You know who he means!" Joan chided him. "I think it's very accurate."

"You and I know because we can read into it what we knew before," Burt said dourly. "He uses too many generalities and inferences. He's afraid to get sued."

"Sure, he has to. None of you guys would back him up!" Joan said.

"Well, he's dragging it out. It's been running for a week now. He knows no more than he did when he first came to see me. He has no solid proof," Burt said negatively.

"I still think it'll do so some good even if it only drives Beatty under a rock where he belongs," Joan stood and went over to the sink. "No one has seen Beatty for three weeks."

Burt stood up and Joan saw him turn white, double over and fall back in the chair. He slumped forward, collapsing on the table.

Joan ran over to him and immediately felt the carotid pulse in his neck. The skin was cold and clammy. She tried to lift his shoulders off the table to get him back in the chair so she could get at his chest but he was too heavy.

She ran to the door and called to JoAnn at the nurses' station, "Code Blue, Dr. Josephson!"

A few seconds later, every nurse in the ICU was in the conference room surrounding Burt. Four of them tried to lift him without success.

"Call maintenance," Joan ordered. "Get those guys up here to lift him onto a stretcher!"

Everyone was milling about, making the small room severely congested. The resuscitation cart, a large red cabinet on wheels with thirty small drawers of medicines and equipment for cardio-pulmonary resuscitation was in the room. It was bulky because of the oxygen tanks and breathing bags hanging from its sides.

People were tripping over one another and no one could get Burt to move. His neck and back were exposed but there was no way to help him in this position. Amidst all this chaos, Burt raised his right hand and waved it slowly. All random activity stopped to watch.

"No code," he groaned slowly. He waved his hand some more, indicating that he wanted people to leave. Joan started pushing people out the door and others followed after them.

Burt pushed himself up from the table and slumped back in the chair. He was still ashen. His eyes were closed and his face twisted in pain.

When the room was empty except for Joan and Burt, three muscular men in the blue uniform of the hospital's maintenance department stood in the doorway. The youngest, with a thick black moustache and curly black hair spoke.

"We got the derrick double parked," he said. "Do you still need us?"

Burt opened one eye toward a young man he knew well.

"How you doin' Doc?" the youth waved.

"Get out of here!" Joan shooed them away.

Joan held Burt by the wrist counting his pulse as she looked at the second hand of her wristwatch.

"Do me a favor." Burt moaned softly.

"What's the matter?" Joan asked worriedly. "Here, let me undo this," she said as she reached under his hefty thick chin to get at his collar to open it.

"Leave that alone," he swatted her hand gently. "Call Dr. Simon."

"What should I tell him?" Joan said, dissatisfied with her role but otherwise at a loss.

"Tell him to get his skinny little ass over here right away," Burt said trying to manage a smile that was cut off by a spasm of pain.

"Dr. Josephson, I want you to get into a bed immediately," Joan said as fiercely as she could manage under the circumstances. "And get out of those clothes so we can monitor what's going on with you."

"You can tell Dr. Simon that my gallbladder just erupted." Burt said disgustedly. "I'll sit right here until he comes."

His diagnosis relieved some of her anxiety but she took no chances. She reported to Dr. Simon that Burt had collapsed, revived and was still having a lot of pain beneath his ribs. Dr. Simon was in the hospital and appeared in the room a minute after she hung up the phone.

Dr. Simon dashed in, concerned. His long white coat was open and flapping. He took a quick look at Burt, who had improved a lot. The pain was much less severe and some color had come back to his cheeks. He breathed without difficulty and smiled at his friend.

Dr. Simon sat down opposite him at the table. He studied Burt's face, eyes, color, breathing, posture, hands and nails. He took this all in to evaluate the urgency of the situation.

"How to you feel?" he asked sympathetically.

"Fine," Burt answered.

"Good-bye, then," Nate stood up, "I'll see you around."

"I'm not fine," Burt waved him back to his seat.

"That's much better," Nate said, resuming his place in front of Burt. "I don't want to hear any bullshit from you or you can get someone else to take care of you, understand?"

Burt closed his eyes and nodded defeat.

"Good! Now let's start from the beginning as if you've never seen me before." Nate took his pen to jot down notes on his new patient.

It was a good way to start with Dr. Josephson. He told Nate nothing that was new or unsuspected. It simply made him realize he was the patient instead of the doctor. From then on, everything went smoothly.

Almost. Burt insisted he could walk over to his room in the other wing of the hospital. He got as far as the door when he doubled up in pain. He conceded to a wheelchair which depressed him considerably. It also made things considerably easier for the hospital personnel who had to take care of him.

He submitted to them without question, advice or directions from him. He would have liked it better if they were less cheerful while they undressed him, stuck him with needles to draw blood, took his temperature and did the things every patient endures. It seemed to him they were having fun at his expense as the doctor looked down the barrel of a needle from the other end.

There were two things Burt insisted upon and Nate Simon readily agreed. The first was that Dr. Simon would take over his practice. The other was that they would wait until Loretta came to work at the hospital rather than calling her immediately.

With the help of Demerol, Burt's pain had eased a great deal. He vomited twice and still felt nauseated. He was lying quietly in bed studying the ceiling tiles when Loretta walked in. He didn't hear her as she walked softly in her crepe soles.

He wore a green hospital gown, and fairly filled the hospital bed with his bulk. His left arm was taped down to a short armboard at the wrist. The IV tubing disappeared under a gauze bandage covering the needle stuck into the vein. He lifted the arm to eye level to stare at the tubing.

"Hello," Loretta whispered.

"Hi," Burt said sadly. He sounded tired because of the Demerol.

"What's a nice guy like you doing in a place like this?" Loretta smiled weakly. She bent over to give him a hug. "Have you seen Nate?" Burt asked.

"No, Joan told me all about it," she sighed.

"Well, it's not too bad right now," Burt said, smiling a little. "There's a rock about this big," he told her, holding up his thumb and forefinger to make a circle.

"Are they sure it's your gallbladder?" Loretta asked.

"Yes," Burt said dejectedly. "EKG is normal. I didn't have any chest pain. They did an ultrasound study and an x-ray. The stone is blocking the cystic duct and the gallbladder is distended. I could have told them that.''

"Are you going to have surgery?" Loretta asked, afraid he would refuse.

"Day after tomorrow." Burt said.

"I'm glad," Loretta said sweetly. "Don't misunderstand. This has been nagging at you for a couple of years. Do it and get it over with.

"Who's doing it?" she asked.

"Alex Fineberg," Burt said.

"Are you still mad at Joe Pastorini?" Loretta sighed with diappointment.

"I'm not mad," Burt shrugged. "We just don't talk to each other, so how can he come in here and ask me what's wrong?"

"Fineberg looks so young. He's almost the same age as Arnold," Loretta complained.

"He's five years older than Arnold and Nate thinks he's a very good surgeon," Burt assured her. "Besides, Joe will be assisting him, anyway."

It made Loretta feel better, but was of little comfort to Burt. He knew Fineberg wanted Pastorini to be there because of Burt's blubberous belly. Fineberg was an excellent surgeon and so was Pastorini. One would need the other to get safely through his thick layers of fat and deep abdominal cavity.

He was much more frightened than he could admit to Loretta. The Demerol depressed him and made him feel euphoric at the same time. He knew his size would give them a problem but trusted their good judgment. The pain was there, the obstruction too severe to put off surgery in hope he could lose enough weight to make much difference.

The next day, the gallbladder series and blood tests confirmed the obstruction. The constant pressure he felt inside would occasionally reach a crescendo. He would then ring for the Demerol.

It took more than an hour and a half for the orderly to shave his trunk from the nipples down to the thighs. He looked like a tree that had had its bark stripped in the middle. Joe Pastorini came around to wish him good luck. He was in and out of the room within a minute. He wasn't trying to make up with Burt. It was just proper.

With the help of Nembutal, Burt slept soundly the night before surgery. He slept well until they woke him at six A.M. to check his temperature, pulse and blood pressure. He left hand and wrist were puffy and swollen. The needle had torn the small vein and the IV fluid had infiltrated through the loose tissue under the skin. The nurse removed the tape and pulled the needle.

His hand felt stiff as he tried to make a fist. After he sat up, he felt much better. The pain was gone. He pressed the right side of his abdomen. There was no pain or tenderness.

He showered with the special bacteriocidal soap the nurse left for him. With most of his trunk shaved, he felt a sense of nakedness that was new to him. The abdominal skin looked very white framed between the black hair at the nipples above and thighs below.

When he had a day off, he skipped shaving, but tomorrow and the next day he would certainly not shave, and his beard would come in thick and black. The after-effects of surgery and anesthesia would make him look like an unshaven drunk. He decided to shave.

"It's the right thing to do," he told the mirror as he applied the white shave cream thickly over his face. "So what if I feel good today? Tomorrow's another day. It's been bothering me on and off for the past two years. The blood tests were a surprise. If it wasn't for—"

He cut himself just below his right sideburn as he pulled the razor down. The blood ran down from the corner of the wound like a red tear until it dispersed in the white soapy foam. He pressed hard against the wound with a piece of toilet tissue.

"I hope Fineberg's hand is better than mine this morning. Now is the time to do it. We can kill two birds with one stone. I never knew so many people wished me well. That's part of it, too. Everyone in the hospital knows I'm having surgery this morning."

"Dr. Josephson," a familiar voice called sweetly.

He stuck his head out from the bathroom. Loretta stood holding a small tray with two syringes on it. She was wearing a plain white uniform made of Qiana that clung to her body. To Burt, she looked like his bride.

"Put that down," he said, "I'll be right out."

He wiped his face and came out nude. Loretta put her arms around his neck and hugged him tightly. In the small hospital room, the bed was only a few steps away. Not much room for maneuvering.

As he carried her, she clung tightly to him with her legs wrapped around his waist. He sidestepped to the door and slammed it shut. Three steps to his right and he had her in bed.

Before laying her down, he pulled the zipper down her back to the crest of her buttocks. She turned one shoulder to slip her arm out of the fluffy sleeve. He kissed her neck, her bare shoulder and then thrust

270

his tongue deeply into her ear. She squirmed beneath him excitedly.

"Burt, you shouldn't," she breathed heavily as she slipped her other arm free. The dress slipped down to her waist. Burt immediately unfastened her brassiere. His head covered her chest as he gently licked her small, erect nipples. She pressed his head to her chest. The perfume she wore excited him. He breathed in deeply, memorizing the aroma. His mouth could devour her small sensuous breast completely.

He tried to pull the dress down below her hips but the cord and the tailored waist resisted his efforts. He reached under the skirt and put his hand down the back of her pantyhose. With her legs still around his waist, his large hands easily reached her round soft buttocks to her soft moist pouch.

His hand came up to the elastic band at the waist. He tugged but it only stretched without moving the panties downward.

"Wait," she whispered in his ear and pushed him away. He leaned back against his heels with his legs bent under him. His pecker stood up and out with flushed exuberance. Loretta stared at it for a moment, surprised by the nakedness of his shaved pubis and delighted by its size and enthusiasm.

She kicked off her shoes, loosened the

silken cord around her waist and wriggled out of the dress and pantyhose in one movement. She got back in the narrow bed where Burt was lying on his side to make room for her. He slid over her.

"Wait, my nurse's cap," he suddenly remembered the flat gauze cap on her head. It was too late and it didn't really matter. Burt started all over again, kissing, nibbling, licking and loving every bit of her. She spread her legs and guided him to her wet opening. He was hot and thick. He had to push to make her even wider. Then he glided gently at first. She held him tighter and pushed his behind, forcing him deeper. He moved faster and faster and she moved in rhythm with each of his thrusts. She couldn't breathe fast enough as he exploded within her. Her head swung wildly from side to side in passionate joy.

It was too soon over, but over just in time. As they lay there together, someone knocked on the door.

"Get up," she whispered in his ear. She was pinned under him. He moved and she jumped up, gathered her clothes and ran to the bathrom. Burt scooted under the covers. "Come in," he said with a cracked voice.

It was Betty Flanagan, the tall nurse with the big nose and stucco-like skin.

"What's going on in here?" she said suspiciously.

"Nothing," Burt said so innocently that no one would believe it.

"I thought Loretta was here. Oh, there's the preop medication," she said pointing to the syringes and needles on the table at the foot of the bed. "Where's Loretta?"

"Here I am!" Loretta said cheerfully as she stepped out of the bathroom.

"Well, hurry up," Betty said. "The O.R. is calling for the patient."

"I'm going as fast as I can," Loretta shrugged indifferently, but winked at Burt.

"I bet you are, but you better give him the medication now," Betty smiled and left.

"Okay, Burt, turn over for me," Loretta said as she picked up the first needle and syringe.

"Anything you say." Burt turned on his belly.

Loretta rubbed his butt with an alcohol sponge. Then she quickly jabbed the needle in. His buttocks tightened as he jumped. The second shot was quicker and less painful; at least he didn't jump.

"I'll be here when you get back," Loretta said sadly. "Be careful. Oh, that's not what I mean," she said and hugged him. She held back a tear.

A few minutes later, two orderlies showed up with a stretcher. Burt was already feeling high from the medication. He greeted them cheerfully.

"How you doin', Bobby?" he said to the one he knew.

"I'm glad you're still awake and can slide over onto this stretcher for us," Bobby smiled.

That was the last thing Burt remembered. The Demerol-Valium cocktail Loretta stuck into him blocked all ambient sensations. It would take a direct question repeated several times to get his attention. His thoughts remained with Loretta in bed. No one knew why he was smiling in his sleep.

He was able to follow directions as if in a trance. He moved easily from the stretcher to the operating table carefully remembering to keep his front covered with a sheet. Even a drunk remembers a semblance of modesty. Fineberg and Pastorini stepped into the room to say hello before Dr. Axelrod, the anesthesiologist, put Burt under. Burt smiled without knowing who they were.

Dr. Robert Axelrod was Burt's choice among the five anesthesiologists at Brady. He was a dour man with a neatly trimmed full moustache. He rarely smiled as if that would disturb the hair on his lip. He was neat and compulsive in and out of the operating room. He also worked very smoothly.

Burt hardly felt the large bore needle enter through the skin and vein. Axelrod pulled it out, leaving the hollow plastic sheath, less likely to injure the vein even after three or four days.

The Pentathol drip was opened. Soon Burt's head sagged to one side in deep sleep. He breathed easily with the black rubber mask over his nose and mouth. Oxygen was pumped through the mask. Then quickly, the mask was removed and the endotracheal tube inserted in less than five seconds. First, oxygen to insure the airway was clear, and then Halothane anesthetic. Burt was gone.

Axelrod wasn't a talker under any circumstances. The three nurses in the room were too nervous to chatter as usual. They all knew Burt Josephson. Despite confidence in Axelrod, Pastorini and Fineberg, they knew anything could happen.

Idiosyncratic, untoward, accidental: all words that meant unexplained and unexpected disaster. It always seemed to happen to a doctor. Perhaps it seemed doctors were singled out for these horror tales because people who witnessed them always knew the patient personally in one way or another. Perhaps it was a curse.

It took two-and-a-half cups of povidine antiseptic to cover the shaved area of Burt's trunk. Even allowing for a double coat, it was twice the average amount.

There was nothing left to do now but

wait for the surgeons. The doors were closed. The spotlight made the wet brown antiseptic glisten on the skin. The two scrub nurses studied the table. All the hemostats, needle holders, large and small retractors, square and round, were there according to their groups.

The circulating nurse who had just finished painting Burt threw all her paraphernalia in the bucket. The only sound was the steady beeping rhythm of Burt's heartbeat on the oscilloscope and the hissing of the respirator.

"That's it!" Alice, the circulating nurse, said.

The other two nurses turned away nervously. Alice had been working there for over twenty years. She was the assistant supervisor. The other two nurses, in their twenties, had worked in the O.R. two or three years. They had experience, but not on anyone they knew as well as Burt.

"Relax," Alice assured them. "It's just another gallbladder."

Fineberg and Pastorini came in tandem through the door. They were about the same height but Fineberg was much thinner. His arms were smooth and unveined, his hands long and delicate. Pastorini was the bull, with heavily veined forearms and short stubby fingers.

After they were gowned and gloved,

Fineberg took the sterile towels from the scrub nurse. He placed four of them so they formed a rectangle running down the right side of Burt's abdomen.

"I was thinking about a subcostal incision last night,' he said to Pastorini as they draped sheets over the towels.

"It's not worth it," Pazstorini said. "You'll be struggling as it is."

"That's what you are here for, to hold his fat gut out of the way," Fineberg smiled under the mask. "You're the one who has to struggle."

The instrument nurse shuddered as she brought her Mayo stand over to the table beside Pastorini. She faced Fineberg, to whom she would be handing the instruments. She held the scalpel with the handle to him.

The belly of the blade was pulled downward from the rib margin, an inch from the midline, to the level of the umbilicus. Fineberg's hand moved slowly and steadily with constant pressure on the blade. He pressed with the other on the white cloth laporotomy pad, while Pastorini did the same on the other side of the wound.

The sure cut plus the pressure on the edges allowed but a small amount of bleeding although the wound was almost an inch deep. Some blood trickled from the edges and ran in minute streams along the palisade of yellow fat beneath the cut skin. It was nothing they had to stop for.

With a second knife, Fineberg deepened the wound. Larger vessels were cut. Pastorini was ready with a hemostat to clamp the bleeders. Almost two inches of fat was divided before he got to the glistening, fibrous sheath of the muscle. He stopped cutting while he and Pastorini tied off the clamped bleeders.

Burt's heavy muscles separated easily. Without thinking about it, Fineberg was helped by the succinyl choline circulating in Burt's blood. Axelrod had injected it earlier and would repeat the injection as the drug's effects wore off.

The peritoneum was opened and the thick walls of the abdominal wound sagged. With the muscle tone absent because of the succinyl choline, Burt's belly was like an open satchel, floppy but full.

Fineberg clipped a towel on each edge of the wound. A large self-retaining retractor that looked like a gleaming metal insect with two long wide legs was inserted in the wound. The two legs were pulled apart along a ratchet and separated the wound edges.

The bowels slithered about in an invisible clear fluid. They looked quite healthy. He pulled them out to examine them by touch.

He saw kidneys and spleen were also normal as he moved his hand through the cavity.

The liver stood like a red-brown mesa overlooking this valley of snakes. It was smooth and slippery from the surgeon's viewpoint. From the inside, it was an overhanging cliff with bumps and hollows where other organs leaned against it. To the left of the liver, which tapered toward the mid-line, Burt's stomach hung like a soft, thick-walled balloon. Some air had been swallowed.

Fineberg asked the anesthesiologist to pass a long thin tube through Burt's nose down to his stomach. He helped position it in the stomach and the bloated bag decompressed. It left a lot more room to work.

The tangle of bowel was covered with a laporotomy pad. Pastorini placed his hand over the lap pad and retracted all the bowel away from the liver. After two days of no solid food, Burt's bowels were collapsed and slid easily away.

The edge of the liver was gently lifted with a curved retractor. After setting the placement of the retractor, Fineberg gave the handle to the second scrub nurse who was standing at his side.

The greenish-black gallbladder popped into view. It was distended with bile and glistened with watery inflammation. That end of the gallbladder was readily accessible. It extended down deeply into a collection of fat that hid some vital structures. It not only hid them, but pasted the cystic artery, veins and common duct together.

"I'm going to start from the top," Fineberg said looking up at Pastorini.

"Sure, I wouldn't go down there yet," Pastorini agreed.

There were two ways to excise the gallbladder at this point. One from above and one from below. Going from below meant getting the cystic artery which was the main blood supply to the gallbladder. With this clamped off, cutting out the gallbladder from its liver bed produced very little bleeding. The danger was that the artery crossed close to the common duct. It was a good way to go if the common duct could be seen clearly, but in Burt's case, the whole area was obscured and matted together with fat.

So Fineberg started from above. With very gentle pressure, he pulled the scalpel blade down the side of the distended gallbladder. A previously invisble film appeared, a fine, diaphanous layer of connective tissue that bound the gallbladder to the liver bed was separated without cutting the muscular wall of the gallbladder.

He stripped this thin connective tissue on both sides, freeing the body of the gallbladder. A heavy clamp was placed at the tip of the gallbladder for traction to pull the organ upward. As he gently pulled, one could see the organ taper to the narrow cystic duct. With a fine gauze sponge he pushed the adherent fat downward, exposing the narrow cystic duct to just above the common duct. The pulsating cystic artery could be seen snaking upward.

Using a series of long-handled clamps with tips at right angles from the stem, Fineberg shut off the blood supply and the remaining attachments of the gallbladder. Pastorini steadied the clamps while he slipped silk sutures around the vessels and tied them off.

Everyone, surgeons and nurses, relaxed, with sagging shoulders and sighs.

The wound closure required great care but any seamstress willing to follow directions could handle it. With succinyl choline relaxing the muscles, there was no tension as the knots were snugged tightly. Once the muscles were approximated, the anesthetics were shut off, Axelrod continued to breathe for Burt until the succinyl choline wore off completely.

Pastorini congratulated the younger Fineberg and he dropped out to let the nurse help him close the skin. He said he would tell Loretta everything had gone well and Burt was just fine.

SEVENTEEN

Burt was fine by all standards of medical art and science. It was only the pain, the worst he had ever experienced, that bothered him. He had nothing to compare it with. This was his first operation and he had had no broken bones. He remembered a childhood toothache which seemed much worse because he thought it might never leave him. In his clouded mind, he accepted the deep burning sensation in his abdomen without complaint.

The dryness in his mouth was much more bothersome. That was the effect of another drug, atropine, which was used to dry all his secretions. That was worse than the abdominal pain. It was combined with a soreness in his throat where the endotracheal tube had been lodged.

There was one side effect of the anesthesia he didn't mind too much. Under light anesthesia, through a combination of decreased inhibitions and increased blood flow, the penis becomes engorged with blood and erect. It doesn't always happen but considering Burt's preoperative state, it was to be expected.

When they moved him off the operating table onto the stretcher, his sheet fell off. The nurses were still talking about it after he was settled in the recovery room. The nurses from the O.R. sent in a scout to get periodic progress reports on the magic wand pushing up into the sheet.

"Burt's doing fine but he needs you badly," one of the nurses told Loretta as she passed through the operating room to the recovery room. They laughed loudly which relieved her anxiety but didn't help her understand.

Burt opened his eyes in response to her voice. He was dopy and drowsy but aware of his surroundings. He looked around at the other stretchers lining both sides of the room. Only one other patient was back from surgery. His slow but growing alertness and awareness of the pain diminished him below. One of the O.R. nurses came to check.

"I knew you could do it, Loretta," she smiled.

Harriet Christopher, the head nurse in the recovery room, was standing on the other side of the stretcher.

"Get out of here," she said to the curious young girl who left giggling.

"What's going on?" Loretta asked a bit flustered because she suspected what had aroused their hilarity. She had barely recovered herself from this morning.

"Don't listen to those jerks," Harriet said. "Here are his vital signs," she said pointing to a pad. "Here's the order sheet. He had Demerol and there's more if needed. D-five and half normal saline running with tetracycline every six hours,"

Harriet finished her report and left Loretta to take care of Burt. She had to check his pulse and blood pressure every fifteen minutes for the next four hours, but otherwise there wasn't much to do. Two hours later he was transferred back to his room. He was more alert than before, so the trip and transfer from stretcher to bed was very painful. She gave him the prescribed Demerol and he slept most of the time.

Using good sense, none of his friends in the hospital stopped by to visit him. The best thing was for him to sleep, letting time heal the wound and dissipate the pain.

Nate Simon stopped in as his physician. The patient was doing well. He checked his color and got a report from Loretta. Fineberg and Axelrod stopped by to see their patient, also. Everyone assured Loretta things would be just fine.

About four o'clock, she gave him another dose of Demerol. He slept more soundly than ever. She had to call their sons in Boston. Before the surgery, they felt there was no reason to tell them. Loretta wanted all her attentions devoted to Burt. The regular floor nurse would respond if Burt needed something. Loretta went down to the coffee shop to grab a quick snack while she called Boston.

She didn't notice the man sitting in the lobby with his nose buried in the newspaper. No one noticed him. There were a dozen people waiting in the chairs and sofas of the lobby.

If anyone had been aware of him, they wouldn't have recognized Dr. Emery Beatty in a toupe. Without his moustache and with the hairpiece, he looked much younger. He wore a short leather workingman's jacket that looked badly worn, jeans and mud-scuffed ankle boots. He was reading Charlie Dresden's fifth article on the notorious "Dr. X."

He was reading it for the ninth or tenth time. He would read it again and again until Loretta Josephson came down as he hoped she would. No one could criticize her for taking a short break.

Beatty hurried up the back staircase at the end of the corridor which opened a few feet from Burt Josephson's room on the second floor. The corridor was deserted. He stepped back in the stairwell when he saw the charge nurse at the other end of the hallway. She went back to the nurses' station. She was out of sight and the corridor again deserted.

Beatty entered Burt's room. He closed the door slowly and softly. He took a few deep breaths as he watched Burt do the same. Beatty stepped forward and stopped to be sure Burt would not awaken.

His hand was wet with perspiration. When he pulled the glass vial from his pocket, it shot out of his hand and landed on the carpeted floor with a thud. It was unbroken and Burt was still asleep. Beatty sank down with his back sliding against the door. His left foot was trembling as he reached for the vial of clear fluid, marked "Succinyl Choline."

The bottle was sealed with thin, pliable white metal over the rubber stopper. This top had a circular perforation that was usually pulled off easily to expose the soft rubber cap.

Beatty's hands shook violently. He stabbed at the metal with his fingernail but couldn't grip the thin metal perforation. His movements were too jerky, the metal stiff but flexible. He stuck the cap in his mouth and pulled against his teeth with a sudden jerk. The thin metal popped up. As it came from his mouth, the sharp-slivered edge cut across his lip. It produced a narrow cut that bled profusely. The red stream flowed down his chin, neck and stained his collar. He ignored it.

His face was contorted. His grimace spread the wound in his lip, making it bleed faster. His nose was heavily creased with lines of distortion.

From his coat pocket, he fished out a sealed packet containing an alcohol swab. He tore the packet and wiped the cap of the vial. It was a subtle but bizarre thing to do. He was trying to maintin good aseptic technique while preparing to commit murder.

With his teeth, he tore the sterile

envelope containing the needle and syringe. Shaking, he got the sheath off the needle. His left hand cupped the vial upside down with his fingers wrapped around as if he were holding the neck of a guitar. He pressed against the wall to steady himself, his right hand moving the needle to the rubber cap.

At the last second, his hand trembled, and he punctured his finger. The movement carried through the skin between a set of digits; the skin was lacerated.

A jagged cut spewed blood down along his palm but he held onto the vial.

He pulled the needle back, stained with blood, and tried again. He coaxed the needle to the thin soft center of the vial and pushed it in. The clear liquid became stained with the blood washed off the needle. The piston was pulled back slowly and the red, murky fluid flowed into the barrel of the syringe.

Beatty stood up by scaling the wall with his hands. He seemed steadier now that he had the weapon loaded, but not completely steady as his hand moved along the wall, smearing blood in broad streaks.

"You bastard!" he whispered at Burt, sleeping and pale.

The intravenous line had a short side-arm with a rubber stopper available to add medications if needed. Beatty found this under the blanket. It was close to where the tubing entered Burt's arm. Beatty injected the paralyzing succinyl choline through this portal.

The injection produced a burning sensation in Burt's hand. He pulled his hand away and opened his eyes. The world was hazy in a narcotic fog. He saw a male figure but the features were vague. His eyes focused better but he still didn't recognize the clean-shaven man with the toupe.

Charlie Dresden burst into the room and stopped short at the sight of Beatty bleeding from the lip and hands.

"What did you do?' he shouted breathlessly.

"It's too late to save him," Beatty sneered, holding the bottle up for Charlie to see.

The door banging against the wall and Charlie shouting awakened Burt enough for him to realize what had happened. His face froze with fear as he could feel his will to move obstructed by some seemingly magical power. He forced his will to work harder which came through in small shallow breaths.

"Code—pho—code—blue—" he struggled. One arm got up a few inches toward the phone and fell back.

Charlie dashed to the other side of the bed. Taped on the phone were instructions to dial 200 for code blue.

Charlie dialed. The operator waited for instructions instead of answering. Ordinarily this saved time on this reserved line. Charlie expected instructions from her.

"Dr. Josephson in room 248, Code Blue," he said desperately. He held the phone unsure of what would happen next. A second later he heard it over the paging system, loud and clear.

"Code Blue, room 248. Attention, Code Blue, room 248."

Lorettt heard it in the coffee shop. She dropped the cup, which smashed on the counter, spraying coffee. She ran down the hall crying all the way back to Burt's room.

Two nurses and an orderly with the crash cart got there first. The nurse on the floor couldn't figure out what was going on from the scene in Burt's room. Burt's eyes were open, staring straight ahead. His color was good and he looked alert. She expected to find an unconscious victim.

Burt still had a little bit of muscle movement. His jaw moved slowly but he didn't have enough breath to speak. He stopped to conserve his movement for whatever small amount of air he could exchange.

"It's Dr. Josephson, he can't breathe," Charlie shouted.

The nurse placed a green nasal oxygen tube in Burt's nose and hooked it up to the wall oxygen source. It did nothing to help

Burt's mechanical problem. He was more terrified than ever, seeing and knowing she was doing the wrong thing. Time was running out, he knew. Soon even the shallow movements of his chest would stop. The precious air just at his nostrils, even at the inside of his throat, would not reach his lungs.

Loretta ran in, out of breath with tears running down her cheeks. She looked at Beatty without recognition but his bloody hands and lip tipped her off that he was responsible. Everyone was just standing around. One nurse had put the EKG electrodes on Burt's chest and this recorded a normal heartbeat.

Loretta tore the vial of succinyl choline from Beatty's bloody hand. She let out a short, screaming gasp, then ran to Burt's side. She pulled the nasal oxygen from his nose. With two fingers, she pinched his nose while her other hand opened his mouth. Her lips pressed hard against his and she blew air from her lungs into his. Her head lifted up and she took a deep breath, held it and blew it down through his mouth again. She repeated this in a slow, steady rhythm for the next two minutes while the others watched.

Dr. Axelrod, the anesthesiologist, came running into the room, still dressed in greens.

"Respiratory arrest," the floor nurse reported to him.

"He was poisoned with succinyl choline by him," Charlie said angrily, pointing to Beatty.

"Laryngoscope," Axelrod pushed his way to get behind the head of the bed. The headboard came off giving him access to Burt. He did it all with measured speed so as not to disturb Loretta's mouth-to-mouth resuscitation.

"The next time she went to Burt's mouth, she felt his lips pucker and his tongue reach into her open mouth just as she was blowing out. She coughed, gagged and lifted her head up.

"You're okay,' she sputtered and bent down to hug him dearly.

EIGHTEEN

Loretta looked weary and crumpled from spending the night in the chair beside Burt's bed. Unshaven and bleary-eyed, Burt looked like he was suffering from a bad hangover. Except for the pain due to his bloated gut when he moved, he didn't complain. He never knew it could be so hard to get out of bed, but he managed to get into a chair with the help of four nurses.

Nate Simon was there, looking cross and offering no sympathy at all.

"I'm taking Loretta home right now," Nate said stiffly. "You're alert enough to fend for yourself. She looks worse than you do."

"That's a good idea," Burt said. "I'm fine, Loretta. Do what the good doctor tells you."

"I'll do as I please," Loretta snapped. "I'm still not sure I want to talk to you, Burt Josephson! You and your stupid friend, Charlie. When is he coming back?"

"He should be here soon," Burt smiled.

"Then I'm leaving," Loretta said in a huff. "I'll be back in a couple of hours. Make sure he's gone!"

"Stay home and rest," Burt pleaded with her.

"No sir, I won't miss giving you one shot in the can if I can help it," she said bitterly.

"You deserve it, Burt. That was a stupid thing to do," Nate Simon said, solemnly shaking his head.

"It was the only way." Burt was exasperated by all this criticism. He grimaced from a mild spasm, hoping to get some sympathy. Loretta and Nate only looked at each other, ignoring his plea.

"You wanted me to have this surgery

anyway, you big phony," he said to Nate, who still looked austere at his suffering.

"You could have had it without exposing yourself to a maniac," Nate said, showing some anger. "Falsifying an emergency is a breach of the hospital rules."

"I was really good," Burt smiled. "I had you fooled, you cockamamy doctor."

"Your actions were disgusting," Nate said.

"Good, give it to him Nate," Loretta urged him on.

"You disrupted the entire ICU," Nate said, pointing a finger at hime.

"It was part of the plan. Without making a fuss, Beatty would never have known I was going into surgery. This way, the news was all over town by five o'clock that afternoon," Burt said.

"It still doesn't excuse Charlie for what he did," Loretta.

"That was my idea entirely. Don't blame him for that," Burt said, demandingly. "I did it to Mrs. Lipton. The least I could do was to do the same to myself."

"With Charlie's help," Loretta said.

"Of course with Charlie's help," Burt said. "Beatty was calling him every day, threatening, begging, even crying—but admitting nothing. After reading his first article, I knew it would be a stand-off. Charlie had nothing concrete to support his allegations in the paper."

"So he talked you into saving his ass from a giant libel suit," Loretta said, still bitter at Charlie for risking Burt's life.

"No, Charlie wanted a libel suit," Burt insisted. "That's why he called Beatty Dr. X. If Beatty sued, he would be admitting he was Dr. X. But Beatty only complained privately to Charlie. Even if he went public, it still wouldn't be enough. I could see that from what Charlie wrote.

"I was willing to risk Mrs. Lipton's life. I didn't fully realize this until I read Charlie's articles. Don't look at me that way, either of you. I needed this operation. Beatty was already mad at me because of that call I made to him. It was easy for Charlie to make him believe I had more damaging information that would hold up in court. He said he was saving that for the final chapter. And it's right there on the the front page: "The Final Chapter on Dr. X.'"

"I heard all that last night," Loretta said. "If you and your stupid friend want to play chicken with a maniac, don't get me involved. It seems to me you were faking that paralysis and almost choked me."

"I wasn't faking and it wasn't supposed to go that far," Burt said, with the terror of the moment returned to him. "Charlie was keeping an eye on Beatty. The disguise didn't fool him. He took his eye off him for a minute to make a call. He'd been watching him for three or four hours. When he came back, Beatty was gone from the lobby. It was a strange feeling," Burt said soberly. "Watching everybody doing the wrong things, paralyzed but awake, knowing what to do for myself but unable to tell anyone. It seemed to go on for eternity. How long did it take?"

"At least seven or eight minutes from the time Charlie called in the code," Nate said more sympathetically. He knew he had come close to losing Burt.

"I never lost total control," Burt said. "I had just a little bit of movement all the time. Not much; maybe I was completely paralyzed for a few seconds. It was hard to tell. Then it suddenly wore off. Maybe I was too scared. With you there," he looked at Loretta, "I was just trying to make it easy for you. Your lips were so sweet on mine."

"Good-bye, Romeo," Loretta said. "I'll be back in two hours. Make sure that Charlie Dresden is gone when I get back!"

"Why didn't the drug work completely,?" Burt asked.

"In the first place, you're a giant tub of lard," Nate said. "He probably didn't give you enough, judging from what was left in the bottle. It was the right dose for an average-sized patient. You should have been paralyzed longer than you were. The other thing was the blood in the bottle of succinyl choline. I don't know how it got there, but the blood was hemolysed, releasing enough potassium to counteract some of the blocking effects of the succinyl choline. I bet you didn't know potassium inhibits the action of succinyl choline."

"You are so smart, Nate. You amaze me sometimes. Would you be my doctor?" Burt said, slipping off the sleep in the chair.

WORLD WAR II
FROM THE GERMAN POINT OF VIEW

SEA WOLF #1: STEEL SHARK   (755, $2.25)
by Bruno Krauss
The first in a gripping new WWII series about the U-boat war waged in the bitter depths of the world's oceans! Hitler's crack submarine, the U-42, stalks a British destroyer in a mission that earns ruthless, ambitious Baldur Wolz the title of "Sea Wolf"!

SEA WOLF #2: SHARK NORTH   (782, $2.25)
by Bruno Krauss
The Fuhrer himself orders Baldur Wolz to land a civilian on the deserted coast of Norway. It is winter, 1940, when the U-boat prowls along a fjord in a mission that could be destroyed with each passing moment!

SEA WOLF #3: SHARK PACK   (817, $2.25)
by Bruno Krauss
Britain is the next target for the Third Reich, and Baldur Wolz is determined to claim that victory! The killing season opens and the Sea Wolf vows to gain more sinkings than any other sub in the Nazi navy . . .

SEA WOLF #4: SHARK HUNT   (833, $2.25)
by Bruno Krauss
A deadly accident leaves Baldur Wolz adrift in the Atlantic, and the Sea Wolf faces the greatest challenge of his life—and maybe the last!

Available wherever paperbacks are sold, or order direct from the Publisher. Send cover price plus 50¢ per copy for mailing and handling to Zebra Books, 475 Park Avenue South, New York, N.Y. 10016. DO NOT SEND CASH.

THE DYNAMIC NEW WARHUNTER SERIES

THE WARHUNTER #1: KILLER'S COUNCIL (729-5, $1.95)
by Scott Siegel
Warfield Hunter and the Farrel gang shoot out their bloody feud
in the little town of Kimble, where War Hunter saves the sheriff's
life. Soon enough, he learns it was a set-up—and he has to take on
a whole town singlehandedly!

THE WARHUNTER #2: GUNMEN'S GRAVEYARD

(743-0, $1.95)
by Scott Siegel
When War Hunter escapes from the Comanches, he's stuck with
a souvenir—a poisoned arrow in his side. The parched, feverish
man lying in the dust is grateful when he sees two men riding his
way—until he discovers he's at the mercy of the same bandits who
once robbed him and left him for dead!

THE WARHUNTER #3:
THE GREAT SALT LAKE MASSACRE (785-6, $2.25)
by Scott Siegel
War Hunter knew he was asking for trouble when he let lovely
Ella Phillips travel with him. It wasn't long in coming, and when
Hunter took off, there was one corpse behind him. Little did he
know he was headed straight for a rampaging band of hotheaded
Utes!

*Available wherever paperbacks are sold, or order direct from the
Publisher. Send cover price plus 50¢ per copy for mailing and
handling to Zebra Books, 475 Park Avenue South, New York,
N.Y. 10016. DO NOT SEND CASH.*